MEISTER ELEMENTARY LIBRARY

Ballet Fever

Betty Cavanna

THE WESTMINSTER PRESS
PHILADELPHIA

MEISTER ELEMENTARY LIBRARY

This work is a revision of the publication entitled
Take a Call, Topsy! © 1947 Elizabeth Headley

All rights reserved—no part of this book may be reproduced
in any form without permission in writing from the publisher,
except by a reviewer who wishes to quote brief passages in
connection with a review in magazine or newspaper.

Published by The Westminster Press®

Philadelphia, Pennsylvania

PRINTED IN THE UNITED STATES OF AMERICA
9 8 7 6 5 4 3 2 1

Cav

6024

Library of Congress Cataloging in Publication Data

Cavanna, Betty, 1909–
   Ballet fever.

   Published in 1947 under title: Take a call, Topsy!
   SUMMARY: Sacrifices, disappointments, hard work,
and joy all become part of Teddi Baldwin's life as she
trains to be a ballet dancer.
   [1. Ballet dancing—Fiction] I. Title.
PZ7.C286Bal   [Fic]   78–3684
ISBN 0–664–32631–5

Chapter 1

"Nervous?"

"Well, a little," Teddi admitted. Her fingers were cold and she could feel in her stomach a familiar flutter of apprehension. She smoothed the bodice of her tutu, then doubled her thumbs into her palms and pressed her hands against her waist.

Miss Heritage made an encouraging grimace and adjusted the winglike sleeve of the ballet costume on Teddi's tanned shoulder. "You'll be all right. It's those babies out there I'm worried about. If little Jill Martin doesn't fall flat on her face—"

Teddi moved behind the dancing teacher and stood on tiptoe so that she could see over her shoulder. From the wing of the improvised outdoor theater she could get only a distorted view of the children's corps de ballet. Jill was at the end of the line nearest her, plump and short and red in the face with concentration. The music seemed to be speeding uncontrollably beyond the child's capacity to catch up with it. But she was so earnest that she made Teddi remember her own early years of dancing lessons.

"One AND two AND three AND—"

Jill's lips were moving in a noiseless count. She had forgotten to smile and her arms waved about wildly. Miss

[6]

Heritage hissed in a stage whisper, "Jill, stop watching your feet!"

Jill's head jerked toward the wing and she straightened hastily. Teddi watched for a moment more, then moved to a spot from which she could catch a glimpse of the shadowy audience seated on folding chairs beyond the footlights. The hospital benefit had drawn a large crowd, most of which had gathered to watch the dancing. The moon, sliding behind a half circle of trees in the background, couldn't compete with the attraction of the arc lights. Teddi took a long breath. To be a ballerina even for the advanced children's class of the Heritage Dancing School was an exciting thing!

The tempo of the music slowed. Miss Heritage nodded. Teddi readied herself for an entrance and a second later was on stage.

She could hear a ripple of approval, like a soft "Ah!" pass over the audience, and she knew, without special vanity, that she made a pretty picture in the frothy ballet skirt. Teddi was small and well made, with blond hair that fell heavy and shining to her shoulders. Her legs were slim and straight and she possessed natural coordination. A dancer could make good use of such traits.

Teddi's round chin lifted ever so slightly as she began to dance. She scarcely heard the labored breathing of the children posed in a half moon behind her as she concentrated on her arms, her hands, her shoulders, her back, her legs and feet, trying to unify them and use them with grace that would seem effortless and natural to the audience below.

As she faced the back of the stage for an instant she could feel the admiring eyes of the corps de ballet upon her, and Teddi's confidence increased. It was good to be alive. It was good to be dancing! More than ever before, as she performed the conventional steps of the ballet, Teddi felt capable and happy and free.

Then, before she had time to do more than sample this

astonishing sensation, the dance was ending and she was back in the wing with the chorus of children crowding before her. She could hear the audience clapping appreciatively and she knew that somewhere out there in the summer darkness were her mother and dad and her younger sister, Jane. She hoped that now her father would feel that the years of ballet lessons had been worthwhile. Never before—because Teddi discounted those early Heritage School recitals—had he really seen her dance.

Miss Heritage whispered, "Take a call, Teddi!" and the girl went back to make the traditional bow.

She smiled without self-consciousness as she looked out at the indistinguishable, upturned faces. Her arms were extended and her left foot drawn back en pointe as she bent her body from the waist. Her hair fell forward and she shook it back, then, flushed and full of triumph, ran to the wing.

Miss Heritage was marshaling her pupils down the backstage steps to the lawn, cautioning them to "Sh!" with her finger held to her lips. Teddi followed and began to shiver slightly in the darkness. Away from the warmth of the spotlights, she felt the chill of the late August night.

"Anybody seen my pink sweater?"

Teddi's question could have been a signal, so quick was the crowding of the younger dancers about her.

"Oh, Teddi, you were wonderful!"

"You're as good as a real ballerina!"

"How did you learn to do so many fouettés?" Jill cut in. "If I did more than two, I'd land on my chin!"

"If you did more than one!" Miss Heritage corrected, and rumpled the child's hair affectionately.

Along with everyone else, Teddi laughed. "I've been studying with Madame Valentin all summer," she explained to Jill. "I ought to be improving *some.*" Then she bit her lip, afraid that her words might offend Miss Heritage, but the teacher had moved on.

"Valentin?" Jill squealed, obviously impressed. "Are you allowed to go to Philadelphia all alone?"

Teddi was amused. "Darling, I'm fifteen, remember?" And Jill, with only eleven birthdays behind her, murmured a meek "Oh."

By the time Teddi had found her sweater and slipped it on, the performance was over and parents were crowding backstage. Mothers of the budding dancers—"ballet mammas" the teachers at Valentin's called them—began to chirp over their offspring like nervous birds. They fluttered around Teddi too, kindly and congratulatory.

"You were lovely, dear. Just lovely!"

"I understand you've been studying with Valentin. Has she such a temper as they say?"

"You were very nice, Theodora. As I always say, dancing's a wonderful thing to teach a young girl poise."

Teddi smiled and made appropriate answers until Mrs. Martin, Jill's mother, sighed and said, "Well, I suppose now that you're going away to school you'll have to give up your dancing. It seems a shame."

A knife thrust could not have been sharper. Teddi could feel herself stiffen as she searched for an answer to a question she had been dodging during the flying summer months.

"I-I—" she began. Then Jill, looking up in adoration, saved her from stumbling into an admission.

"Imagine!" she yearned. "Going away to school!"

Going away to school! As Jill said them, the words were full of adventure, yet they sounded ominous to Teddi's ears. She did not want to give up her dancing and go away. Not even to room with Pat Rutherford. Not even to please Dad. Not even to be introduced to a new and hitherto unknown glamorous world.

"I brought you a coat, dear." Teddi started as her mother tossed it around her shoulders with just a suggestion of an embrace. The two smiled into each other's eyes and Teddi knew that her mother too thought she had danced well. Together they started to move toward the parking area. High school boys, enlisted as helpers, were banging the folding chairs flat and piling them for removal by truck. Teddi saw Rodney Shaw and waved to him and Rod waved back, then seemed to forget his chair-slamming and stood looking after her in consideration. I'll bet if Mother weren't with me, he'd ask to take me home, Teddi thought as she climbed into the backseat of the family car beside Jane and uttered a sisterly "Hi."

"Hi," Jane echoed. "You did swell."

"Did I?" Teddi was interested because she knew she could count on the family to be entirely frank.

Jane's reply was an affirmative grunt. She was at the inarticulate age.

"It looked good to me," Mr. Baldwin mumbled from the driver's seat. "I don't pretend to know anything about dancing, but it looked all right to me."

"Well—thanks, Dad." Teddi's heart leaped at the praise. Maybe, after all, her father would see—

But his next words disillusioned her. "I was talking to Mrs. Rutherford. I didn't know you were planning to room with Pat, Teddi, but I think that's fine."

Teddi mumbled something unintelligible. She could feel her chest tighten, and the buoyancy of success began to disappear.

"The Rutherfords are nice people. Always have been," her father was continuing. "And Pat seems to me like a girl who has her feet on the ground."

Did Dad mean that she, Teddi, did not? Was he still engaged with the idea that dancing was a frivolous pastime, nothing more? Normally Teddi would have teased him about such solid sentiments, but tonight she curled up in the corner of the car seat in sullen dismay. How could she ever make him understand?

Jane sighed. "I wish I was going away to school."

"Were, darling," her mother automatically corrected.

"Were, then. If I went away to school, I might learn to say 'were.'"

"You might learn right here at home," Mrs. Baldwin said.

"But can I go next year?" Jane persisted.

"Let's wait till next year comes."

Jane kicked off her loafers and drew her feet up to the seat, hugging her knees. The expression in her gray eyes became dreamy and she said, including the whole family, "I was reading a book today where the girl—"

"A boarding school book, I'll bet," Teddi cut in. "Mother, you shouldn't just let her *steep* in those silly stories. She gets the weirdest ideas—"

Jane overlooked the slur but said, "What do you mean, steep?"

But before Teddi could reply, her father, turning into the Baldwins' drive, entered the conversation again. "Janey," he said, "hasn't got the priority in this family for wacky ideas."

Because, at the moment, she was feeling unduly sensitive, Teddi took the remark to herself. There should be a school for fathers, she thought—a school where they could learn how their daughters feel about things like—well, like dancing. But then she doubted if Dad could ever really get her point of view. Oh, he was nice enough in his way, and she loved him and all that. She loved the smells of tobacco and soap and leather that clung about him—the very masculinity that seemed to make it impossible for him to understand her.

The car rolled gently into the garage and Jane scrambled out first. "Are there any cookies?" she asked as she preceded Teddi into the house. "I'm hungry."

"I'm hungry too," Teddi admitted. "Dancing's hard work."

Mrs. Baldwin found the cookies and poured two glasses

of milk for the girls, then got a third glass down from the kitchen cupboard. "Dad'll want a snack too, I suppose," she said with a twinkle in her lively brown eyes, so like Teddi's. "Watching a dance recital is hard work for him."

"What did you think of it—honestly now?" Of course Teddi meant, "What did you think of me?" She wanted to hear the unspoken praise with which her mother had greeted her put into words. But she didn't want Jane to think she was conceited, so she phrased the question cautiously.

Mrs. Baldwin was just as careful. "The children were adorable—they always are. They puff and pant and *try* so hard. But I doubt if there's a dancer among them unless it would be that little Follansbee girl. Jill Martin was the funniest."

"And me?" Teddi simply had to ask. "Do you think I've improved—with Valentin, I mean?"

Her mother's eyes met Teddi's squarely. "Yes," she said, "I think your lessons this summer have given you a great deal of sureness and style. I was very proud of you, Teddi."

"Mother," Teddi began, but just then her dad banged through the kitchen door with the two spaniels, Sherry and Flip, at his heels, and she stopped abruptly.

"Sherry's soaking wet," Mr. Baldwin said. "We're going to have to break her of this night hunting. All she does is race through the fields."

"She takes the puppy with her too," Jane said. "Yesterday I saw them both way up near the old Garfield place."

Conversation developed around the dogs, with Mrs. Baldwin and Jane sinking to the floor to tug at the burrs matted in the spaniels' feathers. Teddi was temporarily excluded, and she realized that her opportunity to bring up the subject closest to her heart was lost, at least for this evening. She rinsed out her milk glass, then yawned. "I think I'll go to bed."

"We're all going to bed," replied her mother. "Yes, you

too!" she told Jane sternly. "No more reading tonight."

Teddi ran upstairs, taking the steps two at a time, to be first in the bathroom she shared with Jane. She flung her ballet slippers on the bed and brushed her teeth hastily, then went back to her room and closed the connecting door to the bath firmly. She wanted to be alone.

Slipping out of the pink sweater, she caught a glimpse of herself in the full-length mirror on the closet door. Quickly she did an arabesque, watching her shoulders and arms and the extended leg which seemed to grow visibly in length.

Yes, Madame was right, she had a "good line"—a quality which Teddi knew was indispensable to the classical dancer. But a good line wasn't everything.

Still, Teddi knew as she walked away from the mirror and began to unhook the bodice of her tutu, tonight she had reached an important decision. She wanted, above all things, to go on with her dancing. She wanted to taste again that freedom and power she had felt for a few minutes on stage.

And, the thrust of her chin affirmed, as she wriggled out of the frills of tarlatan, she *didn't* want to go away to school.

Chapter 2

Pat Rutherford phoned first thing the next morning.

"Hi! Want to go swimming? It's a super day."

"If we can go this morning," Teddi told her. "I've got my dancing lesson this afternoon."

Pat sounded provoked. "You and your dancing! Nobody'll be over at the pool this morning. Everybody waits till afternoon."

Teddi tried to be conciliatory. "I'll pack some sandwiches and we'll take our lunch. Then you can stay on. How about that?"

Pat agreed, and they decided on a place to meet. "I've got so much I want to talk to you about!" Pat cried into the mouthpiece. "Do you realize that it's only a month!"

Teddi knew well enough what Pat meant. She put the receiver back in its cradle thoughtfully. How could she ever break the news to Pat that she wouldn't be rooming with her at school?

Then she realized she was jumping to conclusions, and her mouth quirked ruefully. Her initial problem was her father, and he was no easy man to persuade.

But since there wouldn't be a chance to tackle her father until evening at the earliest, Teddi's mind leaped ahead again to Pat. She couldn't remember a time when she hadn't known Pat Rutherford. Their mothers had been classmates at the Sinclair School and Teddi and Pat had been flower girls in the same wedding when they were only four years old. Both had always lived in Spring Mill and had shared the same secrets from kindergarten on.

Teddi knew that much of Pat's happy anticipation at the thought of going away to school was based on the fact that they'd be roommates. Pat wasn't the kind of girl who liked to explore new worlds or conquer them on her own. It was true that of the two Pat was the more dependent, yet Teddi recognized that she gave a great deal too. She gave Teddi loyalty, and friendship that went deeper than companionship. Pat had always been one person Teddi could really talk to, about everything except her dancing. That, for some reason, she rarely discussed.

Maybe, Teddi considered as she stuffed her suit and towel into a waterproof bag, if I could make her understand how important— But at heart she knew that she could never make Pat see that to continue dancing lessons would be a valid reason for giving up going to Miss Sinclair's, which had become a tradition in the Baldwin family, since even Teddi's grandmother had gone there.

Teddi wheeled her bike out of the garage and rode across town to Green Tree Road, where Pat was already waiting, sitting on the top rail of the fence that bordered the Garfield place and chewing absently on a long blade of field grass.

Her face, freckled across the bridge of her short straight nose, brightened when she saw Teddi. Pat had dark eyes that could be very alive, or, when she was bored, equally listless. Her short brown hair curled in warm weather, and today it was clinging to her head like a cap.

"Hot, isn't it?" she said.

"Sticky," Teddi agreed. "I can't wait to get in the water."

They were almost alone at the pool, except for a girl they knew only by sight who was talking to the lifeguard. Teddi came out of the bathhouse first and stood flexing her toes on the edge of the diving board until Pat came down to the water. Then she dove in and swam to the raft, her pale hair streaming behind her.

Pat followed, and pulled herself up on the float. Teddi dove again, turned, and came up to sit beside her.

"I wish I had your figure," Pat said enviously. "D'you suppose I'll ever thin out?"

"You're not fat," Teddi insisted. "Just because you're shorter than I am, and a little bit chunkier, you have an inferiority complex. Anyway, my legs are too long."

"Maybe when I get away to school and start eating that awful food—" Pat started hopefully.

Teddi burst out laughing. "How do you know the food's awful? You're as bad as Jane. You've both read too many boarding school books."

"I have not!" Pat protested, then met Teddi's teasing brown eyes and had to laugh too.

"Mother says she'll bake us cakes or cookies once a month and send them to us." Pat stretched out full length on the float.

"That'll be great," Teddi murmured, feeling like a hypocrite. She let herself down on the warm boards to lie on her stomach, with her head cradled in her arms and turned away from Pat.

"We're going to town shopping on Friday," Pat hurried blithely on. "I want a new coat in the worst way. And some new sweaters—and jeans."

They lay silent then, letting the sun lull them. Pat could make the idea of going to Miss Sinclair's sound pretty exciting, Teddi decided. If she could only do both—continue her dancing lessons and room with Pat too!

But that was out of the question. Mrs. Baldwin had already consulted the school and the most they could promise was the opportunity for Teddi to come down to Philadelphia once a week.

"Once a week is better than nothing, isn't it, dear?" her mother had asked.

"Not for a ballet dancer," Teddi had tried to explain.

But even her mother couldn't take her dancing *that* seriously. She had just smiled.

When the noon whistle blew, Pat sat up at once. "I'm hungry," she announced. Together the girls swam back to the dock and shared the lunch Teddi had packed. Then some of the school crowd began to drift down from the bathhouses, and a group collected around Pat and Teddi to discuss the coming football season, which always made good conversation in late August.

Rodney Shaw was the hope of the incoming sophomore class. "He's bound to make varsity," Bill Bryant, a junior and Spring Mill's best blocking back, told Teddi. "Man, but he's fast."

"We'll have to try to come down," said Pat, "to see a game."

"Down from where?" Bill asked in the lazy drawl he had brought with him from North Carolina.

"We're going up to the Sinclair School—Teddi and I."

Teddi's stomach flipped over uncomfortably. She knew that, even to Bill Bryant, Pat's words carried a certain cachet. He said, "Gettin' too good for the common people?" but there was a touch of envy in his tone.

"If I'm going to get another swim, I've got to go in now." Teddi stood up and started toward the board.

"It hasn't been an hour since you ate," Pat cautioned, but Teddi just grinned back over her shoulder. "With half the football team to rescue me, I'll take the chance."

She did a jackknife off the board, showing off a little because she knew her diving was almost as good as her dancing. Both were arts that required the kind of coordination she possessed naturally. She struck out toward the float with a slow crawl and before she was halfway there another swimmer overtook her. "Hi, Rod," she said, turning over and floating on her back for a minute. "I didn't know you were here."

"Just came," Rod said. "You been here long?"

"Pat and I brought our lunch." Teddi grabbed the float with her hands and brought herself up to a sitting position on the edge with a single twist of her body.

"Heck, I wish I'd known," Rod said. "I've just been bumming around since ten o'clock."

It was flattering to be sought after, and Teddi, wringing the water out of her long hair, looked up to give him a smile. She liked Rod Shaw and she was glad he liked her. He had a naïveté, a forthrightness, that was appealing in a boy who stood six feet and tipped the gym scales at 160. She liked his direct blue eyes and the way his dark hair curled.

Teddi pretended deep sorrow. "I'd even have made you a sandwich."

But here Rod reneged. "I've had your sandwiches. Cream cheese and watercress!"

"We had roast beef today."

"You didn't?"

"No, we didn't." Teddi edged out of Rod's reach as he made a playful grab for her. She slipped into the water, swimming under the surface to come up several yards from the float. "Be seein' you," she called back.

"Hey! Where are you going?"

"Got to go in to Philly," Teddi shouted over her shoulder. She didn't want to mention the dancing lesson for fear of sounding affected, particularly since Rod hadn't mentioned her performance of last night. When she had climbed the steps to the dock she turned again and waved back to him, then said good-by to Pat and the rest of the crowd and went up to the bathhouse to dress.

An hour later Teddi boarded the Philadelphia local in a heat haze that shimmered against the red brick of the station building. But the air-conditioned car was as cool as the pool. Once in the city she scurried through the streets in the shade of the shops and reached the studio with relief.

In the locker room several students of the four o'clock class were already changing listlessly from their street things to practice dress. Teddi pulled tights and a leotard from her locker. She slipped them on, then braided her hair and pinned it on top of her head.

"Hot, isn't it?" somebody asked.

Teddi nodded. "I'll say."

But complaints were few among the dancers, tying back their hair or winding the ribbons of their ballet shoes around their ankles. As soon as the three o'clock class began to break up they started to drift into the classroom to begin their exercises at the barre.

Teddi could remember the first time she had seen the word "barre" spelled. She had always thought of it previously as the English "bar," and like all the French terminology of ballet it had seemed fascinating to her, and different. Actually, of course, the barre was simply a long length of metal pipe, supported at intervals, that ran around three sides of the big, bare room. Beneath it was a lower "baby's barre," but this was never used by the older students.

Teddi took her place in line and the girl ahead of her glanced back and moved up a few inches to give her more room. The pianist sorted through the music on the rack, made a selection, and then turned to talk with one of the students.

Meanwhile Teddi did her pliés, the knee-bending exercises performed in the five conventional positions of the feet. Awkward as this squatting routine looked, she could feel the softening effect on her muscles. By the time the pianist struck the opening chords of the dance music, she was already beginning to warm up.

Then, with the other girls, she fell into the sequence of

exercises that always, at Valentin's, preceded centre practice. She knew them by heart and performed them in careful time to the music, trying to remember the fine points in the use of her body on which Madame had coached them all—shoulders straight, legs rigid, feet well turned out.

The class worked for ten minutes, and then Madame Valentin herself came casually into the room.

The head of the school wore the black tights and leotards of her profession. Valentin was no longer a young woman, yet she carried herself with assurance, and her darting eyes swept the dancers at the barre in a brief, all-seeing inspection. She put up both hands to smooth her hair, too black to look entirely natural, away from her high forehead, then walked to the girl ahead of Teddi and spoke to her sharply.

"In a rond de jambe, Mary, the thigh must be kept quite still." With one hand on the girl's waist and the other supporting her extended leg, Madame illustrated. "You must work for control. It is everything!"

Teddi tried to watch her own control in the big mirror that almost covered the opposite wall. The image confused her and she could feel herself get slightly off balance. Where was the sense of ability and freedom she had experienced last night? As always, before Madame Valentin, she felt like a raw amateur.

The music stopped, Madame clapped her hands and issued some orders in French, and the formal instruction of the class began. For three quarters of an hour, with perspiration running down her cheeks and neck, Teddi gave herself up to trying to perform the movements Madame required.

First the class worked as a unit, then Madame divided her pupils into two groups. She rapped out directions in quick French, then scolded, cajoled, and criticized by turn.

"Pah! There is not a dancer among you! Waving your arms and legs like so many rag dolls." Madame illustrated graphically, and the result was as grotesque as she had intended. "There is a word for the manner in which an

entrechat should be performed. Theodora, what is it?"

Teddi stared at Madame blankly. The unexpected question had caught her off guard and she couldn't seem to collect her wits. Madame fixed her with piercing dark eyes. "Yet you consider yourself a member of the advanced class in ballet dancing. Advanced! Among the lot of you is there one who can give me an answer to a question a mere beginner should know?"

Her eyes swept the class and a slight, sharp-featured girl raised her hand timidly.

"Well, Cecile?"

"Is it 'allegro' that you mean?"

"Allegro. Brisk! Lively! Now that you understand the definition, kindly put it into action. Music, please. We will do that combination again."

For the final five minutes of the hour Madame worked them unmercifully. Try as she would, Teddi couldn't seem to be brisk. Yet she didn't grumble as some of the girls did on their return to the locker room. She mopped her damp face with cleansing tissue in silence, then confessed a troubling question to Cecile Perrine, the little French girl whose locker was next but one.

"I wonder if Madame meant what she said today?"

"Said?"

"That there was not a dancer among us."

Cecile laughed. "Oh, pay no attention. She was just angry."

But before going home, Teddi did an unprecedented thing. She sought out Madame herself, in order to put the same question. She just had to know.

Chapter 3

Lucia Valentin, dressed in street clothes, was quite a different person from the Madame of tights and leotards that Teddi knew. Her summer dress hung loosely on her spare figure, and though she walked with the erect, lithe grace of the dancer, her style was gone.

Teddi got up from the bench where she was waiting in the anteroom and walked toward her. "C-could I speak with you a minute, Madame? It's important, really."

Madame seemed to see her, yet not to see her. She nodded, but her eyes were fathomless. "Why, of course, Theodora. What is it?" She did not suggest that they sit down.

"It's about what you said today—that—that there wasn't a dancer among us," Teddi blurted. "If you meant it—if you really meant that—I've got to know."

Valentin's laughter trilled and she patted Teddi's shoulder. "Child," she said with a shrug, "you must get used to my bad temper. I am famous for it, eh? And today I felt in the entire class such lethargy—such—" She spread her hands in a descriptive gesture. "Oh, I know the weather is hot, but that is not excuse enough. When one works, one must work."

But Teddi felt she was being put off. "I want to know," she insisted, facing Madame squarely, "whether you think I can be a dancer, or whether you don't. If you think I have no talent—or just maybe average ability—I want you to tell me. A lot depends on it."

The dancing teacher seemed to see Teddi at last. "You have a pretty face—much prettier than usual in a ballet dancer. You have a good arabesque. You have balance and you are sensitive to the music. But have you the ability to develop the personality and authority of a first-rate ballerina? It is too soon to tell."

So, in the end, it was a decision Teddi had to make herself, whether to fight for the right to continue her dancing. On the way home on the train, staring into the sunset thoughtfully, she had to face the fact that even if she went on working with Valentin for the next three years, she might find that the freedom of expression which is the ultimate aim of ballet would never be hers. She might never attain the individuality that would set her apart. She might acquire the technical ability but never the necessary artistry to be great.

And Teddi wanted to be a ballerina, not just a part of some professional corps de ballet.

Of course she knew that the corps de ballet must come first. She was endowed with enough of the Baldwin realism to know that there is seldom a shortcut to success. But she did wish, in facing her family, that she might have had Madame Valentin's unequivocal backing. She needed support.

The tree-shaded streets of the suburb seemed pleasantly cool after the city. Along with a clutch of commuters, Teddi walked home quickly. She passed the high school, which dozed away behind its parking lot. She passed the Shaw house, and kept her eyes straight ahead, not wishing to appear interested in catching a glimpse of Rod. She passed little Mrs. Bowers, rocking away the years of her old age on the lawn of her daughter-in-law's house.

Mrs. Bowers called a greeting in her thin, rasping voice and added, "I hear you were lovely last night, Teddi, just lovely," and Teddi thanked her with as pleased a smile as she could muster, hurrying on to turn the corner into Ridge Road.

Square and white and substantial in the softened evening light, the Baldwin house seemed especially pleasant to Teddi as she unlatched the gate in the picket fence.

The cockers ran to meet her, wagging a welcome, but Jane was nowhere in sight, which meant that the family must already have started dinner, which her mother usually served at this time of year on the screened terrace at the back of the house.

Teddi banged through the screen door into the center hall, dropped her handbag on a chair and called "Hi!"

"Teddi? Good! Come on, dear. We've just started."

"Fine. I'll be right there."

Teddi washed her hands in the downstairs powder room, then slipped into her place at the glass-topped table. Jane, already absorbed in buttering a baked potato after her own special fashion, acknowledged her older sister with the briefest of nods, but Mr. Baldwin stopped to serve Teddi and said redundantly, "It's been a hot day."

Anxious to appear cooperative, Teddi agreed with him. "Especially in town."

"You've been in town?" Then Mr. Baldwin remembered. "Oh, of course. Your dancing lesson. Which reminds me, I paid that last bill today. This just about winds them up, doesn't it?"

Teddi looked down at her plate and picked up her fork without answering. She was trying to decide whether the time might now be ripe—

"Doesn't it?" Mr. Baldwin repeated impatiently, as

though he wanted confirmation from his daughter's own lips. "After all, it's time you were getting your things together for school."

"Dad, I don't want to go away to school."

Jane's fork stopped on the way to her mouth and she stared at Teddi incredulously. "You don't—"

Mrs. Baldwin's fingers found the base of her water goblet and she turned it nervously, looking from her husband to her daughter as though she were searching for some way to take the edge from the astonishing statement and conciliate the pair.

Mr. Baldwin simply put down his butter spreader and pushed back his chair. "Don't want to go to Sinclair's?"

"You're nuts," Jane recovered herself to tell Teddi. "You're stark raving mad."

Teddi, feeling the storm already beginning to thunder around her, stiffened. "I can't help it," she said.

"But, Teddi—we've always planned—you've been looking forward to it, I thought. With Pat to room with, and all. Besides, for a college foundation, Sinclair's is—"

The puzzled concern in her mother's voice made Teddi turn to her. "You see, I don't want to go to college either. I know it's heresy, but I don't."

"Then what under the shining sun," roared Mr. Baldwin as he slapped the arm of his chair with the palm of his hand, "do you want to do?"

Teddi met her father's eyes. "I want to go on to high school here and keep up my dancing."

"Dancing!" Mr. Baldwin almost hissed the word and one of the spaniels, peering at the master of the house from behind Jane's chair, shrank back. "Dancing, dancing, dancing! Of all the tomfoolishness I ever—"

"George," said his wife with mild reproof.

"I don't care. There's got to be some discipline in this family." Mr. Baldwin glared at Teddi. "Yes, I said discipline. And the sooner these girls know it the better." His palm slapped the arm of his chair again.

Jane, who felt herself for once outside the maelstrom, was eating a third hot biscuit. She looked up in surprise. "I don't see why—"

But her mother put out a hand and said "Sh," so Jane subsided. Anyway, this was Teddi's show.

Teddi's feet were curled uncomfortably around the legs of her chair. She faced her father, however, with a determination that matched his own. Her round chin jutted out at the same angle as his; her eyes had the same blaze.

"You can *make* me go away to school, but you can't make me want to," she cried. "Why is it any more foolish to want to study ballet than to want to be a—a real estate man?" She picked her dad's own business with more venom than logic.

George Baldwin appealed to his wife. "Marthe—" He talked over Teddi's head in a fashion he had when he was very upset. "There must be some way to make the child see. Ballet! When she could go to one of the best preparatory schools in the country. Your own school! And she's talking about tossing it overboard like that." He illustrated. "Poof!"

"A dancer's life is short and precarious, Teddi," Mrs. Baldwin said in a voice kept carefully level. "On the stage at seventeen, off—when?—at thirty? Even if you reach the top."

"And if you don't," chimed in her father, "Radio City Music Hall—"

"The Rockettes," Jane said, "are no more."

"Be quiet," Mr. Baldwin roared.

But Teddi was watching her mother's eyes fill with hurt disappointment. Teddi knew—had known for a year or two now—how proudly her mother was preparing to send her back to the school she'd loved. Suddenly everything was more than she could bear. Teddi pushed her chair back on the flagstones with a harsh, grating sound and burst into uncontrollable tears.

With a budding ballerina's instinct for the dramatic she cried, "I think you're just trying to get rid of me!" and dashed into the house and upstairs.

"Tears! That's the trouble with women. They always resort to tears!" her father's voice rang after her.

"Theodora!" Mrs. Baldwin called, trying to halt such a display of temperament. "Come back and finish your dinner."

"There's the phone!" cried Jane in the midst of the uproar. "I'll answer it."

In the very act of slamming her bedroom door, Teddi paused. She could hear Jane drawl hello as though no time of crisis existed and then add casually, "Teddi? I'll call her."

Jane came to the foot of the stairs. "Teddi! It's for you."

"Tell them I can't come," Teddi mumbled tearfully. Then curiosity crashed through and her voice became stronger as she added, "Who is it?"

"I dunno. Some boy."

"Rod?"

"I said I didn't know," articulated Jane clearly. "Shall I ask?"

"Wait a minute," Teddi called, as she grabbed some tissues. "I'll be down."

Chapter 4

When Teddi got home from the movies with Rod, Jane was already asleep and breathing softly, one arm flung out across the brown teddy bear which had been her nightly companion for twelve of her thirteen years. Teddi walked quietly past her sister's open door and on to her own room, which adjoined her parents'. This door, she noticed, was significantly shut, though a thin strip of light lay along the hall floor at its foot. From within she could hear the sound of low voices. She stepped cautiously across her own threshold and started to undress.

The discreetly lowered voices droned on. Teddi could hear first her father's rumble and then her mother's fluctuating, lighter tones. Though their words were indistinguishable, Teddi was certain they were discussing her. Not arguing, just discussing. If there had been indications of an argument, she would have felt safer because it would have meant Mother was on her side. This way it looked bad.

Teddi folded back the summer bedspread and slipped between the sheets, lying quietly in the darkness, trying to hear. She almost envied her sister, who had no problems—not even boys! Jane was quite willing to dream away the summer days with a stack of books from the public library, replenished twice a week. She didn't seem to be under any compulsion to *do* things.

"Infatuation. Sheer infatuation!" Her father's raised voice carried for a second into Teddi's room. Then her mother said, "Sh," and the voices retreated to a near-whisper. The muscles of Teddi's neck grew tense.

Why couldn't Dad see? she wondered. If only she could put into words how she felt, she might be able to make him understand. But she wasn't very good at talking to grown-ups, not much better than Jane—to be honest. And Dad was as stubborn as a mule when he wanted to be. It never occurred to Teddi that she had inherited a good deal of this stubbornness herself.

Sighing, she turned over, tucked an arm under her pillow and drew her knees up to her chest. Three minutes later she was asleep.

Rain was driving against the small panes of the bedroom windows when she awoke the next morning. She rolled over, yawned, and listened, because she could tell by the particular noises floating up from downstairs the approximate time of day. In a couple of minutes she decided that Dad had left for the office, which was just as well, that Jane had breakfasted and was playing with Flip, and that her mother was loading the dishwasher. If she didn't hurry, she'd almost certainly have to get her own breakfast. Teddi padded hastily downstairs.

Jane greeted her with a grunt. She was lying on her back on the kitchen floor and Flip was standing on her stomach making pink-tongued attempts to devour her ear. Mrs. Baldwin said, "Your orange juice is in the refrigerator, Teddi. Isn't this a wretched day?"

"Horrible," Teddi agreed courteously, then put her hands around her mother's slender waist and rubbed her face against her back. "Mother, will you scramble my egg?"

The morning proceeded like any other rainy morning, except that Teddi felt an unspoken question in the air, and when her mother suggested that Jane clear out the discarded paper dolls from the drawers of the blanket chest in her bedroom she knew that it meant the two of them would have a talk.

Jane, of course, raised an immediate objection. She was a saver, not a thrower-awayer like Teddi, and she insisted that someday she might want those paper dolls again.

"For what?" asked her mother. "You haven't played paper dolls in three years."

"I just might. You never know."

"*I* know," said Mrs. Baldwin. "There are some empty bags in the garage." She gave Jane a playful slap. "Now get up there and get to work."

While Teddi scraped the last of the dishes Mrs. Baldwin spread newspapers on the kitchen table and got out her silver polish and cloths. She collected the tea service and candelabra from the dining room, the vegetable dishes and platters and ashtrays, then said, "You might take a hand at this, Teddi. I want to talk to you anyway."

Teddi's jaw set, and she prepared herself to make a last-ditch stand, but she pulled out a stool opposite her mother and got to work polishing a teapot with unaccustomed vigor.

For a minute or two her mother said nothing; then she opened the subject. "You're really serious about this dancing, aren't you?"

Teddi nodded. She didn't trust herself to speak.

"I don't think I ever realized—even vaguely—how much it meant to you until last night," Mrs. Baldwin went on slowly. "And then it wasn't anything you actually said. I'd just taken it for granted you'd want to go to Miss Sinclair's. It seemed so right, somehow."

"I'd love to go, Mother, honestly I would, because it was your school, and because of rooming with Pat and all. It's just that I can't do both." How to make her see? "And my dancing's so much more *important.*"

Mrs. Baldwin said, "I think I understand how you feel, but I wonder if you've thought about this enough?"

"What do you mean?" Teddi asked.

"I read a book once about the Maryinsky, the state theater of Imperial Russia, in the days of Pavlova and Nijinsky. I remember how the ballerinas worked, even at the height of their fame. Classes and rehearsals, day in and day out. And these were only the fortunate few. There were others, children swallowed whole into the Maryinsky at ten, to work and sweat for seven long years and still to find themselves unable to make the final grade."

Teddi's eyes dropped but her chin stiffened. This was what she feared, what every young dancer feared, but she didn't want to admit it.

"What does Madame Valentin say about your dancing?" Mrs. Baldwin asked.

Teddi was honest. She rubbed violently at her teapot and answered. "She says I have a good arabesque, and that my looks are in my favor, but that as to being a real ballerina, it's too soon to tell."

"That isn't a great deal of encouragement."

"I know," said Teddi.

"There's another thing. Suppose you did go on to become a dancer—even go on the stage at, say, eighteen. That will be just the age when your friends in college are going to football games and parties, meeting boys they may later marry. You'll be working while they'll be having fun. And you like to have fun."

"I know," said Teddi again, although she couldn't look that far into the future and have anything seem real. She put down the teapot and picked up a covered vegetable dish, jabbing her polishing cloth into the jar of silver polish viciously.

"You also know," her mother persisted, "that there's still a good deal of sweat and tears connected with professional ballet dancing."

Teddi looked up at last. "I don't mind working."

It was the best she could do. She couldn't tell her mother anything of the sense of freedom and exhilaration that real control over her body gave her. She couldn't explain the satisfaction of flying effortlessly through a sequence of steps that three months ago she had managed to perform only with the utmost concentration. Somehow she felt sure that her very inability to put her feelings into words was losing the day. Then her mother surprised her.

"Suppose we make a bargain, Teddi," she said. "I may as well tell you that Dad, especially, feels that this—this absorption in dancing is partly because you're young and have a lot of energy. He and I had both hoped that over this summer you'd get it out of your system and be ready to settle down a little."

"Out of my system?" Teddi frowned. "I've had six years of it and—"

Her mother waved off the interruption. "I started to talk about a bargain—an agreement between us. Dad and I decided last night that if you were really serious about this, we'd be willing to give you another year's grace and—"

Teddi was on her feet. "You did?" With the silver dish in one hand and her polishing cloth in the other she flung her arms around her mother's neck. "Oh, Mother, you're a lamb! I know you had to talk Dad into it. I can't thank you enough!"

Mrs. Baldwin smiled back at her ecstatic daughter, and if there was a touch of ruefulness in the twist of her lips Teddi didn't see it. Her mother held her off by the shoulders and said, "Just don't let me down."

"Let you down? What do you mean? I'll work like—"

"I mean more than that," Mrs. Baldwin said, turning back to the table full of silver. "If you find that your dancing is living up to your own expectations, tell me. If you're losing interest in it, tell me that too. It's so hard to help another person—even a daughter—plan a life. Dad and I just want to help you avoid any grave mistakes."

"But I know my dancing isn't a mistake, Mother! It's the thing I want to do more than anything else in the world. Haven't you ever had anything you felt that way about?"

Mrs. Baldwin's laugh ran up the scale. She leaned back and her eyes held an expression—almost teasing—that baffled Teddi. "Yes," she said slowly, "I have."

Teddi was rather surprised. "You have? What?"

"When I got out of college," her mother said, "I was offered a traveling fellowship to go abroad and study art. I wanted to go in the worst way."

"Then why didn't you?"

"Because I wanted to do something else even more. You see, I got married instead."

Teddi was appalled. "But you could *always* get married, and to go to Europe—"

Again her mother's laughter trilled. "Wait till I tell George that!"

Teddi carried the silver over to the kitchen sink and rinsed it under hot water, trying as she did so to revise her lifelong impression of her father. As she had told Pat not long ago, she had always considered her dad the solid-citizen type, and now to try to imagine him as a young man whose glamour could compete with anything as thrilling as a chance to study abroad—

Pat. The name smote her belatedly. Then her mother put her thought into words. "Have you thought about how you're going to break this news to Pat? I'm afraid she's going to be pretty disappointed."

Teddi nodded. She was more than afraid; she was certain. "I'd better go over and see her right away."

She started across town toward Pat's house with mixed emotions. Why hadn't she prepared Pat for this possible decision, she wondered now, instead of keeping the whole thing to herself? But she knew the answer. Because Pat had never understood about her dancing. And probably never would.

A horn honked and a car pulled in toward the curb, brakes squealing. Teddi turned her head, bent against the rain, and recognized Bill Bryant, leaning out of the window of his old VW and calling, "Want a lift?"

"Do I!" Teddi ran toward the car thankfully, shaking herself like a wet puppy. Bill handed her a folded newspaper as she clambered in. "Better hold this on your lap," he drawled. "She's got a leak in the roof."

With an intermittent stream of water falling past her nose, Teddi explained she was on her way to the Rutherfords'. "You going anywhere near?"

"To the very door," Bill lied with southern courtesy. "And what brings you out on this fine summer day?"

"Urgent business," Teddi told him. "But urgent."

Bill dropped his rebel colonel pose. "Got time to stop off for a Coke?"

Ordinarily Teddi would have been flattered, but today she shook her head. She felt as she did when she went to the dentist and wanted only to get the ordeal over with. "I'm late already, Bill." She tried to put sincere disappointment into her eyes.

"You're a fraud, Teddi Baldwin," Bill told her, but he grinned when he said it and obligingly dropped her at the Rutherfords' drive.

Pat was upstairs in her bedroom, and shouted, "Come on up!" when she heard Teddi's voice in the hall. She was sitting on the floor, surrounded by most of the drawers from her bureau, the contents of which had been dumped in mad disorder on the rug.

"I'm trying to sort things out for school," she said when Teddi appeared in the doorway, "and you never saw such a bunch of junk—"

"Everybody's doing it," Teddi said with false gaiety.

"Mother even has Jane working. It must be the weather."

Pat glanced over her shoulder to contemplate the weather, then looked back at Teddi's wet bare legs. "You didn't *walk* over here?"

"Bill Bryant gave me a lift." Teddi dropped to her knees in front of Pat and sat back on her heels. "I simply had to see you."

Pat misinterpreted the remark. "I know," she nodded, her eyes sparkling. "I'm so restless I don't know what to do. And I think of a thousand things I'm just dying to talk over with you and then when I see you I forget them. Do you feel like that?"

"I—" Teddi started, but Pat had jumped to her feet.

"There's one thing I must show you!" She pulled a big box out from under her bed, and turning back the top flaps, began probing away at some crumpled tissue paper. "Aunt Lucy sent it for the two of us." She came up with a flowered cup. "A tea set! Isn't that quaint?"

Teddi took the little cup between her thumb and forefinger and examined it without actually seeing it at all. For the second time in twenty-four hours she could feel her eyes blur with tears, and without looking up she simply blurted out the blunt fact, "Pat, I'm not going away to school."

Pat looked at her incredulously. "You're not *what?*"

Teddi raced on. "I'm going to stay here and go on with my dancing. I feel awful, telling you this way, so late and all." She looked down again at the flowered teacup forgotten in her hand and tried to explain. "It isn't that I don't want to go. I do. But I just can't do both. And you'll find another roommate, somebody—" Overwhelmed by a mixture of regret and sentiment, Teddi stopped to brush the back of her hand across her wet cheek.

"You're crying!" Pat sounded disgusted. "I think you're out of your mind, throwing away a chance to go to Sinclair's for—"

"Girls!" Mrs. Rutherford's familiar voice floated up the

stairwell. "Want to come down and have some sandwiches and iced tea for lunch?"

"You bet," Teddi called back, feigning enthusiasm. As a matter of fact, she found that she was rather glad to follow Pat down to the breakfast room. Perhaps time and food might mellow her friend's first indignant and scornful reaction.

Mrs. Rutherford, a plump and placid woman with a shock of graying hair, was already seated at the table, sipping tea and turning the pages of the morning newspaper. She glanced up and nodded a welcome to Teddi, whom she accepted as practically part of the family, then went on reading while the girls settled themselves on the bench opposite her.

Teddi picked up a tuna fish sandwich but she couldn't seem to swallow the first mouthful. Pat's dark eyes were still so stormy and hurt it seemed impossible that Mrs. Rutherford should not notice. Conversation, at best, was sporadic, and instead of feeling better Teddi became more miserable by the moment. She had been so intent on her own affairs that she had never stopped to realize her decision to give up Sinclair's would seem almost traitorous in Pat's eyes.

Searching for a way in which to lighten the tension, Teddi focused on a picture on the theater page. "Who's that?"

Mrs. Rutherford's eyes glanced up the column she was reading to the photograph of a man in a black velvet jerkin and tights, caught as he performed what only Teddi recognized as a ballotté.

"Justin Falk," Mrs. Rutherford said, consulting the caption. "Formerly of the Ballet Theatre in Paris, who is coming to this city to instruct at the Lucia Valentin School."

"I think men dancers are sissies," sniffed Pat.

Mrs. Rutherford raised her eyebrows. "Not necessarily," she said, folding the single newspaper page and passing it across for Teddi's further perusal.

There was certainly nothing sissy about the dancer pictured here. For the first time Teddi looked down at the strong, sharp features and hard-muscled body of a man who had acted as danseur to a number of famous ballerinas.

"Justin Falk," she repeated. "An interesting name."

Chapter 5

"Justin Falk!"

The name was on everyone's lips at the Valentin studio when Teddi went in for her next lesson.

Ballet mammas whispered it with raised eyebrows and heads appreciatively nodding. Aspiring dancers, chubby and innocent in their first soft shoes, shrilled it with a question. "Who's he?"

Cecile Perrine, sitting on the locker room bench next to Teddi and wadding her toes with lamb's wool, spoke the name breathlessly, her dark, slanting eyes star bright.

Madame Valentin gave the name the ring of authority when she announced it to the advanced class.

"Justin Falk will be with us for the winter. He is coming from California the first of next month and I am expecting him in the studio the fifteenth of September." She paused for effect, her glance sweeping the attentive faces. "It will be a great honor to work with Mr. Falk. He will choose from among my advanced pupils those who he considers have special promise."

A murmur swept the resting dancers but Madame clapped her hands sharply. "Attention! Centre practice." Her crooked finger beckoned to a diminutive redhead.

"Coco, you here." She pointed to a spot on the floor. "Mary, here. Theodora! Cecile! Sarah!" Briskly she arranged the class.

"Have you seen his picture?" Mary whispered to Teddi as Madame's interest passed on to the pupils still waiting to be assigned to places. "He's simply divine!"

Never was there such a furor in the dressing room after class. What the dancers did not know of Justin Falk they conjectured. He could do the lifts in *Swan Lake* as well as Nijinsky—well, almost! He was demanding, more demanding than Madame herself, and he was leaving Hollywood because the motion picture directors were too independent. He was young. He was not as young as he looked—that was a wig in the newspaper picture. He was a Russian. He was not—he was an American.

Teddi went home with her head in a whirl and tried out the great announcement on the family. They were gathered in the living room when she arrived, Jane arranging Flip's long ears like hair beneath a resurrected doll's cap and Mr. and Mrs. Baldwin sipping their before-dinner glasses of sherry.

"Guess what! Justin Falk is coming to teach at Madame's."

Teddi's dad did no better than the youngest of the beginning dancers at Valentin's. "Who's he?" he asked.

Jane presented Flip for family inspection with no regard whatever for her older sister. "Doesn't she look cute?"

Mrs. Baldwin did her best with, "Haven't I seen his name somewhere?"

Teddi struck a dramatic pose, shook her head wearily and sighed. "He's practically the greatest dancer in the United States, that's all."

"Well," commented Mr. Baldwin, anxious to get on with an office anecdote he had been telling his wife, "that's fine."

Jane had removed the doll cap and was trying out the effect of Flip's long blond ears pulled to the top of her head in an upswept hairdo. "Dancing, dancing, dancing," she muttered.

Teddi turned on her. "What did you say?"

"Nothing."

"Children!" chided Mrs. Baldwin, and Teddi turned away. There was no use trying to talk to the family about anything important. They simply didn't understand.

Oh, Mother was all right. She at least made an effort. But Dad and Jane were just dumb—stubborn dumb. Teddi threw herself across her bed and leaned her chin in her hands. She felt very much alone.

But not for long. The phone rang twice before dinner, and each time it was for Teddi. Jo Anne Turner had heard from Ginny Smith who had heard from Pat Rutherford that Teddi wasn't going to Miss Sinclair's after all. Was it true? Well, wasn't that just marvelous, because they needed her in the worst way on the sophomore hockey team! Teddi tried to explain that she wasn't sure she'd have enough time for hockey, but Jo Anne wouldn't take no for an answer. She talked on and on. Then Ginny called to say she was having some of the girls in to lunch next Tuesday—sort of a farewell party for Pat—and could she come?

"I'd adore to," Teddi said blithely and felt a small pang of jealousy. "What time?"

"One o'clock, if that's all right?"

"That's just fine."

"Pat's simply crushed," Ginny babbled on, while Mrs. Baldwin called from the dining room to please hurry, "that you're not going to be rooming with her. I don't see how you have the courage. I don't really! To give up Sinclair's, I mean. When half the girls in Spring Mill would give their eyeteeth to get away to school!"

"Teddi."

"All right, Mother, I'm coming. Look, Ginny, I'll call you back." It was a convenient escape.

Of course she never did call her back, for which Teddi

apologized profusely when she arrived for lunch on the following Tuesday, to find Pat looking anything but crushed in a new wool blazer which was too warm to be worn on the last day of August but so smart that she couldn't be blamed for wanting to show it off.

Pat was cordial on the surface but cool underneath. She seemed to talk to Teddi as much as to the rest of the girls but the pleasant intimacy they had shared together, the glances and smiles that spoke, were now lacking. Teddi felt uncomfortable and a little sad. She and Pat had had disagreements before, but never a real estrangement. She wanted desperately to get back on the old basis, yet she didn't know how.

As she ate her salad and potato chips little things kept floating to the top of her memory. The time, back in pigtail days, when she and Pat had shaken hands solemnly and sworn to be "best friends." A night they had spent together —one of many but memorable because they had discussed, far into the small hours, every possible ramification of the all-important subject of boys.

"Teddi, come back!"

Teddi started, then grinned in apology.

"You're the worst daydreamer!"

"I'm not, really." Teddi sawed at her lettuce and blushed because she had been caught off guard.

Eventually the conversation rolled to Spring Mill subjects, for in spite of its enchantment, Miss Sinclair's was only a dream for all the girls but Pat, and life at home was bound to go merrily along. School was opening right after Labor Day, the girls who had been away at the seashore or the mountains were coming home again, football practice had already begun on the athletic field behind the high school, and a hint of fall was in the air.

"Does Rod Shaw know you're not going to Sinclair's?" Ginny asked Teddi.

"I don't know. Why?"

"He was having a Coke with Claire Woodward yesterday afternoon. I just wondered."

"Claire Woodward? Why, she's in my sister's class. Eighth grade."

Ginny laughed. "She *was* in eighth grade, you mean."

Teddi remembered that Claire had been at the house with Jane several times. A little blonde with china eyes and a halo of hair like a doll's. A breathless voice. Sure! But to imagine that youngster, or Jane, being old enough to interest Rod or the other boys—

The younger generation provided Teddi with food for thought all the way home. For the first time she began to consider Jane as a possible part of her own world. After all, she wasn't much more than a year younger. Yet her interests seemed so different. She seemed so wrapped up in her books, and the dogs, and making collections of things. But boys?

The idea seemed even more absurd when she came upon Jane herself, jeans rolled to the knee, feet bare, sitting on the back lawn combing the spaniels with frowning concentration.

"Sherry's been off in the fields again," she announced. "She's full of burrs—the sticky ones."

"Why don't you cut them out?" Teddi suggested.

"Yeah, and wouldn't Dad love that!"

The cockers were Mr. Baldwin's dogs. Sherry, the five-year-old, was his gunning companion, but little Flip seemed to show none of her dam's taste for the field. She was Jane's pet and that was about all.

Teddi sat down on the grass and reached out to stroke the puppy, who was eyeing Sherry's predicament with considerable interest.

"I've been over to Ginny Smith's for lunch."

"Mmhm."

"Party for Pat," Teddi said, not knowing quite how to conduct a conversation with Jane, whom she usually ignored.

"What 'ju have to eat?"

Such a *childish* thing to ask! But curiosity got the better of Teddi and she decided to finish what she had started. She repeated the menu and was favored with a "Golly!"

Teddi leaned back on her hands and yawned. "They were talking about a friend of yours—Claire Woodward."

"Oh, Claire." Jane put down the comb and started pulling Sherry's hair away from the burrs with her fingers.

"Do the boys like her?" Teddi casually asked.

Jane frowned. "Boys? I guess so. Sure."

"I mean does she have dates and all?"

"Dates?" Jane began to wriggle. "I don't know. I guess so." Suddenly she sat back and looked at Teddi directly. "Say, what are you getting at?"

Teddi tried to look both innocent and aggrieved. "For heaven's sake," she said, getting to her feet, "can't a person even conduct a conversation?" She attempted to wither Jane with a look. "What do the girls in your crowd talk about? Paper dolls?"

She turned on her heel and flounced into the house, but out of the corner of her eye she could see her younger sister still looking after her as she slammed the screen door.

Teddi walked straight upstairs to her room and got out of the striped cotton dress she had worn to the luncheon and into a pair of shorts. Then, because it occurred to her, she began doing her pliés. Madame had said that every professional dancer performed these limbering exercises several times a day.

Besides, it would be well to be in top form when Justin Falk arrived to take over. Teddi never for a moment doubted that she would be among those chosen. Wasn't she attractive? Couldn't she dance as well as practically anybody in the class except Cecile? And Cecile, with her thin, dark face and enormous eyes, wasn't half as easy to look at.

Teddi squatted, raised, squatted, keeping her feet in the first, closed position, then the second, open one. She felt a little creaky in the joints and she persevered for a good fifteen minutes, until her mother ran upstairs and tossed a letter on Teddi's bed.

"Goodness, I didn't realize it had taken me so long to shop. Here's a letter from Aunt Dora. Get Jane and shell the lima beans for me, will you?" Mrs. Baldwin cried.

Teddi tore open the envelope as she walked downstairs. There was a check in the fold of the single sheet and she looked at that first. Fifteen dollars and made out to Theodora Baldwin! Then she read Aunt Dora's characteristic hasty scribble.

Teddi dear,
    Spend this, belatedly, for your birthday, which must have been back in June. Maybe you'd like to get tickets for the New York City Ballet. I hear it's coming to Philadelphia next month.
        Affectionately,
        Aunt D.

"Look, Mother, isn't Aunt Dora a lamb?"

Mrs. Baldwin, unpacking groceries from a cardboard carton, took time out to exclaim. "Isn't that just like Theodora, sending you a birthday check two months late?" she laughed. She adored her younger sister, but thought it was Jane she should have named after her, not Teddi. Jane and Dora were both the absentminded lovable type.

"The New York City Ballet!" Teddi was intoning. "Now how do you suppose she knew?"

Mrs. Baldwin laughed again. "Dora knows everything. That's her business." She added, "And after all, she's right there in New York."

Teddi sat down on a stool at the kitchen table, reached

for the colander, and tore open the bag of lima beans. "Fifteen dollars. That will buy two tickets, won't it, Mother?"

"It should."

"Would you like to go with me?" Teddi asked.

Flattered, Mrs. Baldwin smiled her thanks but said, "Oh, I think you should take one of your own friends. Isn't there somebody you owe?"

Teddi thought. "Nobody," she decided, "except Rod Shaw. He took me to the circus with his family last spring. But that was a long time ago."

Beans dribbled into the colander as Teddi discarded empty pods. She couldn't see her mother's amused expression. She was absorbed by another consideration. Would it be clever of her to ask Rod right now, when his interest might be on the verge of wandering—or would it look too planned?

Then suddenly, without any reason except youthful resiliency, her mind snapped back to the beans she was shelling and she looked at the growing pile of pods in shocked dismay.

"Hey!" she cried, as one betrayed into doing more than a proper share. Kicking back her stool, she made for the back door and shouted, "Jane!"

Chapter 6

School started with a rush and a bustle. Teddi shared with the rest of the sophomores a new sense of prestige and a feeling of responsibility in extracurricular activities. She let Jo Anne Turner talk her into coming out for hockey practice and was astonished and flattered when, on the very first day, Miss Whiteside, the coach, suggested that she might perhaps make the varsity.

Only two other sophomore girls were thus singled out, Jo Anne and Cora Banks, a big, hard-hitting fullback. Jo Anne put her arm around Teddi's shoulders and hugged her. "Oh, Teddi, imagine! We might even get a chance to play in the Franklinville game."

Miss Whiteside overheard and smiled encouragingly.

"Never can tell," she said. "Of course it's going to mean some hard work. You'll be in competition with juniors and seniors who have a good deal more experience than you. And another thing. We're clamping down on practice cuts this year. Three and you're out—even if you're the best hockey player in Spring Mill High."

The sparkle of anticipation died in Teddi's eyes. "What days do we practice?"

"Mondays and Wednesdays, with a game scheduled every Thursday. That way it won't interfere with Friday football," Miss Whiteside said.

Teddi hesitated only a moment. Then she said bluntly, "I can't do it."

Jo Anne looked astonished and Miss Whiteside raised her eyebrows. "No?"

"I've got dancing lessons Mondays, Wednesdays, and Fridays," Teddi explained, though somehow she felt silly, admitting that she considered her dancing of such concern that she would give up a chance to play varsity hockey. "I can get to the Thursday games but I'll have to see them from the sidelines," she went on, trying to put it lightly.

"I guess you will," said Miss Whiteside flatly, and turned away.

"But, Teddi!" Jo Anne was sincerely shocked.

Teddi shrugged, turning stubborn. "I can't help it," she said.

Yet to give up the chance to play varsity hockey was more of a sacrifice than Teddi would admit. She knew she was fast and accurate and that her timing was precise, all qualities developed to a fine degree by her ballet work. The senior who had played right wing on the varsity last year had put on weight over the summer; she was bound to slow up. That night Teddi dreamed of the triumph of taking over her position.

But the next day when the girls said, "Look, Teddi, can't you give up your dancing lessons until after Thanksgiving? That's all it would mean," Teddi shook her head.

"I'm sorry. I'd *love* to go out for hockey. But I just can't." And although she tried to explain, she knew the girls felt she had let down the entire class. Teddi Baldwin was a popular girl but just how far did she think she could go? Where was her school spirit?

It seemed, in that first ten days, that everywhere Teddi turned she met frustration. She was nominated for a class office and had to refuse because class meetings were always held on Monday afternoons. Because she was nimble and quick and good to look at she was invited to try out for cheerleader, but the time they would need her most would be at the Friday football games.

"I'm sorry," Teddi had to say again.

And she didn't enjoy saying it. She was dismayed at the coolness with which some of her own crowd began to treat her. "I think Teddi Baldwin's getting plain peculiar," she overhead a classmate say.

They'll get over it, Teddi told herself. She began to look with unexpected sympathy on the less popular girls in her class, and took more trouble to be friendly than before. She was no longer carelessly certain of her social status. Peculiar? An ugly word.

One night Mr. Baldwin was out at a Rotary meeting and Mrs. Baldwin was reading in bed when Teddi came padding into the room in her bare feet, her hair wound up in loose, fat curls. She smelled of soap and water and talcum powder, and her mother sniffed approvingly as Teddi curled up on the foot of the bed. "What now?" Mrs. Baldwin asked with a smile.

Teddi told her about everything that had been happening, the hockey, the class officership, the cheerleader bid. "It isn't that I don't want to do things," she wailed. "I do! There just isn't enough time."

"Of course there isn't," Mrs. Baldwin agreed.

"But what am I going to do?"

"You've made your choice, Teddi, unless you've changed your mind about your dancing?"

Teddi shook her head.

"Then you'll just have to weather a certain amount of disapproval at school."

"But why can't the girls *understand?*" Teddi wanted to know.

Mrs. Baldwin sighed and thought for a minute. "Wanting to do something as much as you want to study dancing," she said finally, "is an adult sort of reaction. Not many girls in high school feel that way about anything. They're naturally puzzled and a little resentful. They can't help it, any more than you can help being you."

Teddi's eyebrows gathered in a frown but she could appreciate that her mother had touched on the truth. She was trapped by her own decision. Fuming silently, she bit her lip.

Marthe Baldwin leaned forward and patted her daughter's hand. "You'll work things out," she said staunchly. "And remember," she teased, "your troubles are only beginning. If you intend to be a second Pavlova, you'll be practicing every spare moment before very long."

Teddi groaned and thought of her uncompleted homework. "You make everything sound just dandy." She let her shoulders sag wearily. "I'm going to bed."

But once in bed, Teddi couldn't get to sleep. Her mind raced like a squirrel on a treadmill, never really getting anywhere but in frenzied chase of a thousand and one details.

She must remember to tell Mother that her ballet shoes wouldn't hold up much longer; wouldn't it be well to have a new pair before Justin Falk arrived? How many days now? She started counting, slipping over to the world of ballet from the world of school with a scarcely perceptible jolt. Goodness, the fifteenth was next Monday. It seemed almost too soon. She became filled with such nervous anticipation that she could feel herself trembling. She could only remember having experienced a similar sensation once before, when she had her first real date, with Bob Lafferty, and she was so afraid of doing something wrong that her teeth chattered in anxious fright.

Bob Lafferty. Honestly! Hadn't she been a child? She thought of his freckled, serious face with something approaching disdain. Bob was nice enough, but dull—hardly a Bill Bryant or a Rodney Shaw.

Teddi hadn't seen much of Rod since the opening of

school, yet that wasn't unusual. Their homerooms were different, because the initial letters of their last names were at opposite ends of the alphabet, and then there was football practice and all. Still, she decided, she had better check up on Rod.

Teddi turned her pillow and hugged it to her with a heartfelt sigh. So much to do. So little time. That French translation unfinished. Teddi wished she didn't have a broad streak of her father's conscientiousness. It would make life less complicated.

In the morning, at the breakfast table, her mother tore a section from the entertainment page of the *Inquirer* and handed it to Teddi. "Here's what Dora was talking about."

Teddi continued to butter her toast as her eyes glanced over the movie listings and lighted on the more thrilling announcement:

ACADEMY OF MUSIC
ONE WEEK ONLY
New York City Ballet

The toast was momentarily forgotten. "I've got to go Friday," she said after a minute. "Friday they're doing both *Swan Lake* and *Paganini*."

Mrs. Baldwin looked mildly disturbed. "Wouldn't Saturday afternoon be better?" she asked. "Dad doesn't like you to be out too late at night."

But Teddi shook her head. "Saturday's no good. And anyway, Friday's not a night before a school day, Mother, please!"

It was a winning argument. "Well, if Dad will pick you up at the station—" she said, relenting. "After all, if you're taking Rod, I suppose it will be all right. He's always been a responsible sort of boy."

"I *hope* Rod's going with me," Teddi said. "I haven't asked him yet."

She met Rod on the way to school that same morning.

He rode up casually from just behind her on his bike, braked to a halt on the outside of the pavement, and fell into step.

"Hi," said Teddi, and smiled.

"Who hoards the phone in your family, you or your kid sister?"

Teddi was immediately defensive. "Why?"

"Tried to call you half of last evening. Busy, busy, busy. One of you gals must have a lot to say."

"Oh, that was Jane talking to Claire Woodward." Teddi wasn't sure Jane's conversation had been with Claire but she wanted to see if any expression would cross Rod's face. None did.

"You know Claire," Teddi pursued.

"Oh yeah! The little blonde." Rod grinned, showing even, white teeth, and nodded wisely. "She's a comer, that one. Give her a year or two!"

Teddi let her breath out in considerable relief. A year or two was a good deal of grace. She was just ready to broach the subject of the ballet when Rod said, "Say, we're getting off the subject. The reason I called was to see how about a movie with Jo Anne and Jim right after the game Friday?"

"Next Friday night?"

"Sure. There isn't any game today. You know that. Anyway, our whole family's going to Uncle Ed's for the weekend. Leaving before supper tonight."

"Oh," Teddi said, then stopped. "There's only one thing," she went on after a few seconds. "Next Friday night I was going to ask you to go in to Philadelphia with me. Aunt Dora sent me money for seats to the ballet, and I thought I'd invite you to go, because you took me to the circus and all."

Rod's face fell but he tried to be polite. "That'd be great, Teddi. I mean, it's awfully nice of you and everything. But couldn't we make it some other night? I mean this will be my first varsity game. If the coach puts me in, that is. But he says he will. He's as good as promised."

"I don't see what the game has to do with it," Teddi demurred.

"Well, I mean it would be sort of fun to celebrate. A movie with the gang—you know. I just mean the—the ballet sounds sort of highbrow and serious—"

Teddi frowned.

"Oh, well," Rod ended up weakly, waving his right hand in the air above the handlebars of his bike, "you know what I mean—"

"If you don't want to go with me, Rod, all you have to do is say so," Teddi said rather haughtily, because she could feel that she was on more certain ground than she had anticipated.

"It isn't that," Rod denied.

"And as for the ballet being serious"—Teddi tried a new tack—"it's more—well, more *sophisticated* than the movies, but it certainly isn't supposed to be an *ordeal*. Goodness, Mother says the Russian czars thought it was the best entertainment in the world."

"Oh, I'm sure it's great—" Rod began again, in a tone intended to mollify. "It's just that—"

"Look, Rod," Teddi interrupted, "I'm not begging you to go. There are plenty of other people." She indicated with a large gesture that Spring Mill was full of them.

"But I'd *like* to go. Honest I would." Rod rose to the occasion with belated manliness. "I think it's swell of you to ask me." He managed a fairly convincing grin.

"Well, that's fine then," said Teddi, melting. The high school loomed ahead and she felt that the denouement of this little act had been reached just in time.

Chapter 7

Justin Falk didn't make his much-heralded appearance at the Valentin school on Monday the fifteenth after all. Madame explained to the advanced ballet class that his plans had been changed but they might expect him Friday. Teddi's face reflected her disappointment. Too much was on the books for Friday—the ballet with Rod, the first football game of the Spring Mill High season, and now this.

Frankly, she had been planning to skip dancing for once and go to see Rod play in his first varsity game. It seemed quite necessary that she should do this—a turn-about-is-fair-play sort of gesture. But of course Justin Falk's delayed arrival changed everything. Teddi tried to plan how she could get home from dancing class in time to change, bathe, eat dinner, and be ready to start back to town with Rod by seven o'clock.

That it would be a tight squeeze was certain, but her mother was cooperative and promised to meet her at the station with the car. Friday, fortunately, dawned crisp and Octoberish, so that the weather didn't add its special complication to the overcrowded day.

At school the conversation dwelt exclusively on football. The halls buzzed with talk of the afternoon game, the lunchroom rang with it, and Teddi discovered that Rod, as a fledgling member of the varsity, had attained new status in the eyes of the girls in her crowd.

Teddi herself shone in reflected glory. She was the girl Rodney Shaw was dating.

"Let's sit together at the game," Ginny Smith suggested to her. "You and Jo Anne and me."

It took some courage to say, "I'm not going." Jo Anne and Ginny both looked at Teddi openmouthed.

"Not going?"

"No, darn it. I've got dancing."

"But can't you skip it just this once?"

"I was going to," Teddi admitted, "but there's a new ballet instructor coming on from California and this is his first day. I've got to be there."

Nothing—nothing in the world short of a case of the flu or the death of a member of the immediate family could be considered an excuse for missing the first game in which Rod Shaw would play. Teddi could see the verdict written large upon her friends' faces. This final foible was too much!

If, on top of this encounter, Teddi had been forced to admit her defection to Rod himself, she doubted that she would find the courage, but luckily their paths didn't cross once during the afternoon.

With the dismissal of her last class Teddi ducked out of school and hurried to the station in the opposite direction from the crowd streaming to the football field. This, she told herself as she boarded the local train, is really giving up *everything* for art.

She could envision the start of the game as the houses of Spring Mill dropped out of sight behind her—the helmeted, cleat-shoed boys readying for the kickoff, the referee's whistle, the momentary quiet in the stands. Why, she wondered, fretting, did she always seem to want to be in two places at once? Why couldn't she be satisfied with one life or another and not endlessly grasp for both?

Then, after the three-block walk to the studio, the world of the dancing school enveloped her, and it seemed the most natural thing under the sun to be sitting beside Cecile on the locker room bench tying her ballet slippers.

Together the girls walked into the big practice room, went to the barre and began to do their pliés. Cecile was a great deal more excited than Teddi about the arrival of the new master and Teddi knew that it was because the little French girl wasn't being torn two ways. Ballet was her only world.

Teddi worked as steadily as Cecile but her mind was distracted. The late afternoon sun that came slanting through the dusty windows to gild the bare wall reminded her that the game must be approaching the half. She wondered if Rod was playing—she did hope he was! She wondered if Spring Mill was winning and if Jo Anne and Ginny were missing her—she was afraid they weren't.

"Class," called Madame, who had entered the room unnoticed by Teddi, "attention!"

Standing at the barre, the girls relaxed. Cecile alone was unable to resist turning to crane her neck and see if the famous young maestro was waiting in the hall.

Then Madame made a blunt announcement that sent the red blood of angry frustration surging to Teddi's cheeks. Mr. Falk had been detained again.

For the rest of the afternoon Teddi thought only that she could have been at the game all the time. Then there would have been no excuses to make to Rod. She danced carelessly, and she didn't even mind terribly when Valentin criticized her arabesque.

"The heel," Madame rapped, "raised. The hip in."

Sullenly, Teddi tried to comply.

She poured out her grief to her mother the moment she got off the train. "I feel so—so *thwarted*," she cried.

"Thwarted," replied Mrs. Baldwin as she started the car, "is the one thing I'd say you weren't." Then at once she started to talk about arrangements for the evening. She didn't really like the idea of Teddi and Rod being in the city so late at night.

"Look," Teddi sighed, "Rod's a big guy. He can take care of me."

"I don't doubt that, but you're both children, really," Mrs. Baldwin hurried on. "I've looked up train schedules and I think you should just be able to make the eleven fifteen home. Dad will meet you at the station here. I've talked to Mrs. Shaw and it's all understood."

"Talked to Mrs. Shaw!" Teddi was shocked and aggrieved. Treating her like a baby! But there wasn't time to get into an argument about it. They were turning into the drive and there was too much to be done in the mere hour that remained before seven o'clock.

Teddi was still eating her dinner when Rod arrived. He looked scrubbed and shining and all dressed up, and over one eye he wore a significant strip of adhesive tape.

Immediately Teddi thought, the game! It seemed incredible, but she hadn't even asked Jane the score, she had been in such a flurry to get ready on time.

Fortunately Mr. Baldwin rose to the occasion. He grinned at Rod in man-to-man fashion and said, "Well, I see you tied 'em, eh?"

"Yes, we did, sir." Rod grinned back, and unconsciously his hand went to the adhesive tape.

"Get a little cut up?"

"Just a scratch. Somebody's cleat."

Jane, who had been sitting silently and gazing at Rod in awestruck admiration, breathed, "It was a wonderful game!"

Teddi slipped out of her chair and went to the hall for her coat. She glanced at herself in the mirror over the

Hepplewhite table and came back to the dining room. "We'll have to hurry or we'll miss our train," she said urgently.

Rod had to tear himself away from Mr. Baldwin and Jane. They were all talking at once now, and Teddi gathered that it had been quite a game. Rod was so full of it he was ready to explode. His blue eyes were sparkling and he walked with a jaunty sense of well-being. Teddi knew instinctively that this was no time to tell him she hadn't even been there. On the way to the station she just let him talk.

"Man, at the half I thought we were ditched. They'd been really rattling the bones of our backs, the way they blocked and tackled all through the second period. And after those two touchdowns in the first quarter. Zowie! I didn't think we had a prayer."

Teddi clucked sympathetically. "I can imagine."

"And was I scared green when Coach told me to go in! Honest, Teddi, I could hear my teeth chatter."

"You're kidding."

"I am not. And my hands were like dry ice. I mean it. Then what did Ted do, first off, but call that fake buck lateral. We'd only practiced it twice, and I never thought it would work, and for that matter neither did most of the other fellas. When we split the Dalesford line for two first downs I was the most surprised guy this side of Punxsutawney."

"I'll bet," said Teddi.

"Did you see the real buck lateral though? That was slick. When Evans took the ball from Johnson and tossed it out to John Allen, that was really smooth."

Teddi grunted something unintelligible. She was wondering how to tactfully break the news that she hadn't seen the game.

"And when he hit the five-yard line. Man, oh man!"

They were turning into the station parking lot, and far up the curving tracks Teddi could see the headlights of an approaching train. "That's ours, I think," she said.

The two of them ran the last few yards and climbed aboard without tickets. Rod was still in a football trance when he paid the conductor, and on the short ride to Philadelphia he gave Teddi a play-by-play description of the entire second half of the game.

Teddi simply didn't have the heart to interrupt Rod's monologue. He was reliving every moment of the afternoon, and anyway she wanted him to get it all out of his system so that he could settle down and give a little attention both to her and to the ballet.

They walked from the station to the Academy of Music, around City Hall with its high statue of Billy Penn enveloped by the gathering night, and on south down Broad Street. Teddi was listening to the football story with one ear now. Words like "punt" and "defensive" and "penalty" occasionally made a fleeting impression but she found herself becoming absorbed by the city at night. The lights, as always, lent enchantment to a picture that was drab by day. As the bulk of the hoary old Academy loomed ahead, Teddi could feel a thrill of excitement chase down her spine.

She fumbled in her purse for the tickets, and inconspicuously handed them to Rod. She was rather proud of the price of $5.50 printed on their faces but she wasn't so pleased with the words FAMILY CIRCLE. Somehow that sounded entirely too homey, not a proper place to sit when one had a date.

They turned up Locust Street to the side entrance, and with a number of other people, some middle-aged, some young, climbed the endless stairs. They finally reached the semicircular hallway and picked up programs from a big wicker basket set atop a pedestal.

Their seats were around at the side, too far around. When they had climbed down the steep steps into them Teddi found that they were sitting practically on top of the stage. They were high up, too. Below them was the balcony with its boxes, the dress circle, and the orchestra.

"Anyway," Teddi said, feeling that for $5.50 Dad should have been able to do better but trying to console herself, "they're on the first row."

Rod was impressed by the vastness of the Academy, which he had never been in before. His eyes roved up the gilt and cream pillars to their pediments. "Corinthian," he pointed out proudly. They had been studying the Greek forms in school.

A group of schoolgirls swarmed down the steps and into the row behind Teddi and Rod. A man with a thick foreign accent said, "Pardon," and edged past them. The orchestra tuned up and the conductor entered.

"The first ballet is *Swan Lake,*" Teddi told Rod, who had not consulted his program. She wished the opener had been one of the costume pieces for Rod's sake—something more masculine and vigorous in tempo. She smiled encouragingly, then forgot Rod completely as the curtain rose.

There was no one on the vast stage, with its worn boards powdered with rosin. A single crowned swan moved rather jerkily across a moonlit lake near the edge of a suggested forest. A young prince who had come with friends to hunt swans entered, and the simple story of his romance with the Swan Queen began.

To Teddi the symbolism was familiar. She could excuse the smudgy backdrop and the wooden swan whose base was distinctly visible from where she and Rod sat. The setting was nothing, the dancing everything. When the Queen of the Swans appeared Teddi caught her breath because the performance was as crisp and frosty as the Queen's tulle ballet skirt. Here were posés, the pirouettes, the fouettés that Teddi had practiced so often, done with faultless grace and timing.

She loved the dance of the Little Swans, who were linked together by their arms, and watched with parted lips their gay, brisk pas de chat. Too soon the unwelcome sorcerer appeared and spirited the Swan Queen away. Too soon the Prince, unable to break the spell that bound his love, fell fainting to the ground. The curtain met, parted with the applause, drew together again, and the lights went on.

"Aren't they marvelous!" Teddi breathed.

Rod looked puzzled. "Is that the kind of stuff you're studying?" he asked.

Teddi nodded.

"I'll be darned."

Teddi herself had never before seen *Paganini,* the fantastic ballet concerning the masterful violinist, which was next on the program. From above the stage where she and Rod were, a lot of the weird and spectral illusion was lost. They could look down over the heads of the dancers who screened the musician's death couch, see one dancer replace another as the spirit of Paganini, and get in on a lot of stage business which from a lower level would not have been apparent.

By the time the curtain was drawn again Rod was squirming. "Man," he said with a frown, "wouldn't you think they'd learn something from the movies? That shift-around sure was lousy."

Teddi was incensed. She felt as though she had been personally attacked. "You're supposed to be looking at the dancing, not bothering about details." But though she wouldn't admit it, she could see what Rod meant.

After the intermission the prima ballerina and her partner danced. Teddi tried to explain how important they were, but to a boy who had never heard the names they were just two other dancers.

Again Teddi was enchanted. The pair danced the pas de deux from *Giselle* with utter assurance, a flare such as she had never before seen. And the pallid, exquisite ballerina did the most intricate turns with precision and understatement that Teddi could appreciate. With the rest of the house she applauded them for three curtain calls.

"Now that," she told Rod, "is tops. Even if you don't know anything about ballet, you can tell, can't you?"

Rod still remained a little puzzled. "They were good," he admitted, "but they might have done a lot better if they'd put themselves out."

Teddi was amused. "That's exactly right," she said with surprise. "It's their timing. They seem to end their steps just before they're really finished. They never overdo."

"Yeah," agreed Rod. "I guess." Obviously, he felt more and more out of his depth.

Teddi consulted her program again. "I'm glad they're ending with *The Blue Danube*," she said. "You'll love this." And because the lights were dimming, she couldn't see Rod's expression. It was just as well.

The curtain parted to disclose a scene in a Viennese park, where a handsome hussar is torn between his interest in a charming young girl and the worldly dancer who was a former love. The lilting Strauss music was familiar and as the story leaped, rotated and pattered on its way, Teddi became enrapt.

Rod, by this time, was yawning. It had been a long evening at the end of an exciting day. He couldn't sit still for the final curtain calls and was on his feet while the theater was still dark. "Let's get going," he said.

Reluctantly, Teddi allowed herself to be hurried away. She was still under the bewitchment of the ballet when they reached the street.

"I wish they had encores like they do at concerts," she murmured. "I could watch dancing like that all night."

"I'll still take the movies," muttered Rod. The muscles of his legs were beginning to ache and the cut above his temple throbbed.

Teddi fell back to reality with a bounce. "Well, you could at least be polite about it."

"I'm sorry," Rod mumbled, sounding anything but contrite. He yawned again, openly, and started to walk with such long strides that Teddi had to trot to keep up.

They hurried along in silence until Rod said, "I want to get a copy of a late edition of the *Bulletin,* so I can see if they've got anything about the game."

Teddi didn't reply. The spell of the ballet was fading fast under Rod's indifference. Football, football, football—it was all he could think about! She'd heard nothing but football all the way to town and she did not intend to listen to it exclusively all the way home. It was more, she decided, than time for her to take a turn.

"Wait till I tell Cecile I saw just about the most famous dancer in the world."

"Look, Teddi, be reasonable," Rod persisted. "How many people know anything about ballet in comparison to the number of people who go to the movies?" Then, before she could reply, he hustled her through an entrance to the station and over to a newsstand. Walking toward the steps that led to the train level, he was already folding the *Bulletin* at the sports page.

Once seated on the train he studied the newspaper avidly. Finding his name in the small print of the lineup he had to show it to her.

L. E. . . . . Shaw

"Boy, does that make me feel proud!"

"I didn't know you played end. I thought you always played halfback," Teddi said, then bit her lip.

Rod looked at her. "Didn't you see the game?"

It was a rhetorical question, not really serious, and Teddi could have covered her slip if a slow flush hadn't mounted from her neck to her cheeks.

"Say, I don't believe you were even there."

Rod's stare was so searching, so full of indignation, that Teddi couldn't meet it. "Well, what if I wasn't?" she asked, leaping to the defensive. "Football isn't the only thing in the world!"

Chapter 8

With an abandoned heave that ripped the sheet and blanket loose from the foot of the bed, Teddi turned over. She opened her eyes warily and knew at once it was Saturday. The atmosphere of the house was different, quieter. Then she became conscious of a gnawing in her stomach not induced by hunger and she remembered that she had had a fight with Rod.

She closed her eyes again, turned on her side and pulled the pillow down under her cheek. The pillowcase felt cool and pleasant but the sensation in her stomach persisted. Like a premonition of disaster, it made her uneasy. She tried to go back to sleep.

But in spite of herself, Teddi began to relive that dreadful train ride home. She knew, with a sense of personal guilt, that if she had deigned to explain the real reason why she had had to miss the first game of the season, Rod might have understood. As it was, the whole evening had ended miserably. She could remember each invective they had hurled at each other, Rod against ballet and Teddi against football, until they had been reduced to chilly politeness on the trip from Spring Mill's station in Mr. Baldwin's car.

Teddi turned again, trying to shut out the memory of Rod's uncompromising back as he walked quickly up his own drive. Being carted home like a baby, no wonder! But she knew this last to be just a weak attempt to excuse herself. The quarrel was her own fault, not the family's.

The bedroom door opened a crack and a cold nose thrust itself against the back of Teddi's neck. There was a scrabbling sound and Teddi reached out to pin a small wriggling body firmly to her stomach.

"Flip," she said.

Flip swiped her nose with a pink tongue. The plumed tail wagged faster and she nibbled at Teddi's chin. "You're a lucky baby," Teddi told her. "You don't have worries."

There came a sound of water running in the bathroom and Flip's ears pricked. In a second she squirmed loose and was off the bed in a flying leap to make ecstatic rushes at Jane's bare feet.

Teddi could hear her sister's scolding grunts as she brushed her teeth. Then Jane giggled uncontrollably as Flip's tongue tickled her toes. "Let me alone, Flip. Flippy, don't! Teddi, call this puppy!"

"Here, Flip." Teddi stretched, abandoning the idea of further sleep, and began to tumble the spaniel on the quilt, rumpling her swinging ears. Maybe if she treated this like any other Saturday morning, she could forget about Rod.

But not for long. Jane, in green and white striped pajamas, the legs rolled high above her knees, came in to perch on the footboard of Teddi's bed.

"D'ju have fun last night?" she asked.

Teddi yawned deliberately, patting her open mouth with the back of her hand. "Mmhm," she murmured, making her wide eyes a little bored.

Usually this would have closed the subject, but apparently this morning Jane felt uncommonly communicative. She hugged her knees and rocked a little. "I think Rod's smooth."

Teddi took the compliment unto herself but discounted it. "Just because he plays football—" She let the remark go unfinished. Her tone of voice said enough.

"You should've seen that game. It was some game!"

"Since when have you become so interested in football anyway?" Teddi asked, faintly annoyed. "Last year you wouldn't even buy a season ticket."

"I'm in high school now," Jane said artlessly. Then she looked at Teddi with careful consideration. "I don't think you appreciate Rod."

Coming unexpectedly from Jane, and especially this morning, the remark hit Teddi full force. She put her head back against the pillow and laughed without great conviction. "So now I don't *appreciate* Rod!" she mimicked.

Her tone was just supercilious enough to put Jane in her place as the kid who didn't know enough to come in out of the rain, let alone discuss her older sister's boyfriends. Teddi knew she was being cruel when she saw Jane stiffen and flush, but she had to protect herself. "Rod Shaw's not the most important boy in Spring Mill High, you know," she hurried on. "Just because he's made the varsity doesn't mean I've got to go around calling him 'Mister.'" She slid out of bed on the far side and rescued one of her scuffs from Flip's sharp teeth.

Then she swept into the bathroom with a show of indignation that was meant to baffle Jane still further, and when Mrs. Baldwin called, "Girls! Breakfast is ready!" she walked down to the dining room with a languid step.

Of course her mother had to greet her with the question "Did you have a good time last night?"

"All right."

Mrs. Baldwin raised her eyebrows. "Didn't Rod like the ballet?"

Teddi shrugged, knowing that Jane, who was squeezing her grapefruit with sublime indifference to good manners, was also watching her covertly. "What Rod Shaw likes or doesn't like," she said, "is of complete indifference to me.

He's just a narrow-minded"—she considered—"a narrow-minded egotist."

"Them's harsh words," Teddi's father chuckled. "I guess the toe dancing must have been a tee-total loss."

Mrs. Baldwin, from the other end of the table, shook her head at her husband and Teddi finished her breakfast in offended silence. Why did everybody seem to be against her this morning? Why couldn't she at least have had a family that understood ballet?

A family like Cecile Perrine's, for instance? From what Cecile had told her, the Perrines followed the progress of ballet the way Dad followed the World Series. There was a family for a girl who took dancing seriously! And that reminded her of something.

"Mother," she said as she helped carry out the dishes, "there's a girl I've gotten to know in dancing class, Cecile Perrine. She wants me to come home with her for dinner some night. May I tell her yes?"

"Where does she live?"

Teddi wasn't quite sure. "In the city somewhere."

"You find out where," Mrs. Baldwin said calmly, "and we'll see."

Teddi began to tell her mother about Cecile. It took her mind off Rod. She described her, making her seem more interesting, more French and dark and intense, than she really was. Even Jane lent an ear to Teddi's monologue, for all she professed to scorn anything connected with the ballet.

"She's read everything about dancing and the theater," Teddi explained. "Simply *everything*. Her family give her the most marvelous books for Christmas. No wonder she knows so much!"

"If you'd rather have books about ballet than new ski pants—" Mrs. Baldwin began, but Teddi was racing on.

"Of course dancing is her whole life. She never even

thinks about anything else. She says it's got to be that way."

"I think that sounds silly," Jane cut in.

"Well, who was asking you?"

"Teddi! Children!"

As the day wore on, Teddi felt more aggrieved and misunderstood. She was sorry she had flared up against Rod at the breakfast table, letting the family in on what could have been kept a private quarrel. She began to look forward to school on Monday, when she might be able to make her peace. For, to be honest, dancing was far from being *her* entire life. Boys and school played a very important part. But when Monday came and Rod sailed by her in the hall without so much as a glance, Teddi, refusing to be outdone, practically walked over him in history class with her head held high in the air.

As Teddi waited for the 3:20 to town, which was late, she wished she had been less high-handed. She would miss having Rod to take her around. Already the subject of the class party was beginning to come up in the lunchroom at noon. Although the committee hadn't been chosen yet, the situation gave Teddi pause. If Rod didn't ask her to go, who would?

Almost, today, she could wish she had gone off to Sinclair's with Pat after all. Then, she thought, all her problems would be solved. Or at least they would be new ones. Teddi climbed aboard the train when it finally jerked into the station, plopped down in the nearest empty seat, and sighed.

The train was very late indeed by the time it reached town. Teddi scurried up the street toward the studio, dodging in and out among the pedestrians, and got into the locker room to find it already empty. The minute hand of the wall clock jerked forward to rest on four while she was still kicking off her shoes.

Madame did not like latecomers. Teddi whipped her sweater over her head in haste and reached for her leotard.

From the adjoining room she could hear the opening bars of a familiar piano selection. Her fingers fumbled with the ribbons of her slippers. Hurry, hurry, hurry—sometimes Teddi thought that was all she ever did.

As inconspicuously as possible she slipped into the studio, scampered to the barre, lifted a leg, and tried to look as though she had been there all the time. Today she was lucky. Madame had not yet entered. Then Teddi remembered to ask the girl in front of her a question, and the girl answered with a quick nod.

So Justin Falk was actually here!

Cecile certainly must be excited. Teddi's eyes found her along the barre and noted her straining back, her nervous glance at the clock. Beads of perspiration stood out on the little French girl's forehead. She was evidently determined to be supple before the master arrived.

Even the stout pianist who was Madame's most treasured assistant seemed full of anticipation. Teddi wondered what this famous Mr. Falk would be like and hoped that his delayed entrance wouldn't prove an anticlimax. After all, there was only the newspaper picture to go by. For all she knew he might be old and bald. Makeup could do remarkable things.

But the man who walked confidently into the room behind Madame with the smooth, easy stride of a dancer was in need of no makeup to conceal defects. A whisper of approval swept the waiting girls. Backs straightened. Eyes shone.

"Mr. Falk." With a sweep of her hand Madame Valentin introduced him.

Mr. Falk nodded, and Teddi noticed that his black hair had a tendency to curl. He stood easily before them, slim-hipped and lithe in a pair of chinos, his sport shirt open at the neck. With dark, widely spaced eyes he swept the room and Teddi could feel her self-confidence begin to evaporate.

"Good afternoon," he said gravely, with a voice that was as quick and certain as his walk. Then he turned to Madame. "Today I should just like to watch."

"Certainement." When Valentin was excited she always lapsed into French. She clapped her hands as a signal to the pianist and called for the routine sequence of exercises at the barre.

With Justin Falk's eyes darting along the row of dancers, Teddi tried to concentrate on her technique, but she felt heavy and awkward, as self-conscious as she had on the occasion of her first Heritage School recital. Like a first-year pupil's, her legs and arms seemed wooden. This would never do!

Then Madame marked out sets and Teddi was relieved that she was placed on the back row. With an inconspicuous place in the grouping she no longer felt so ill at ease, but now that she wished the new instructor's eyes would seek her out, he seemed interested only in the dancers toward the front.

At the end of half an hour the important announcement of the day was made. Mr. Falk himself, at the next session, would consider each dancer individually and choose those to be included in his advanced class. He nodded again, coolly, impersonally, and left the room.

For the remainder of the period the girls worked feverishly. Each of them, now that they had seen Mr. Falk, now that they knew he was young and attractive and had a dynamic personality, wanted to be included in his class. Madame, scolding and cajoling them, helped to build up his prestige.

"You dance like poodles!" she threatened. "Not one of you will Mr. Falk choose!"

But Teddi and the rest knew better. This was no group of novices; these were advanced pupils in a professional school. There were a number of good dancers among them, girls who might make ballet a career.

"Work!" Madame begged of them. "Concentrate! You must do better!"

In the locker room after class Cecile sat on the bench beside Teddi hugging her knees. "He is wonderful, isn't he?" she sighed. "My mother is right. She keeps telling me what a privilege it would be to work with a man like that!"

Teddi straddled the bench and pulled on her shoes. "Would be? This time next week you'll be saying 'is.'"

Cecile clasped her hands. "Oh, I do hope so. I'm going to practice and practice and practice!"

Teddi had to laugh. "You've only got two days," she teased, "and you'll have to go to school. You won't have much time."

But Cecile was planning to utilize every spare minute. "This is important," she insisted. "It's about the most important thing that's ever happened to me."

Chapter 9

Jane looked up from the book she was reading. She was lying on her stomach in front of a slow-burning fire and Sherry's head was cradled in the curve of her back.

"All I've been doing," she said to Teddi, "is take telephone calls for you."

Teddi still wore her coat. Her eyes were smudged with weariness and she was tearing open a letter addressed in Pat's familiar handwriting. Now that she was home again, the excitement of Justin Falk's arrival was beginning to wear off.

"Uh," Teddi grunted, sinking down on the living room love seat. "Who called?"

Jane rolled over, dislodging Sherry. "Mrs. Rutherford, and will you call her back please." She began ticking them off on her fingers. "A girl—I didn't recognize her voice—and she said never mind. Ginny Smith—she wants you to call too. I guess that's all."

"O.K."

"Well," complained Jane, "you could at least say 'thanks.'"

"Thanks."

Jane returned to her book, and Teddi walked toward the

phone, reading her letter as she went. Pat wanted her to come up to Miss Sinclair's for a weekend. That would be fun, she thought. "Sometime in November, before Thanksgiving," Pat suggested.

Teddi called Mrs. Rutherford first. Pat's mother simply wanted to chat about a similar letter she had just received. "I think it would be lovely if you could go," she told Teddi. "Pat misses you, I'm sure. Actually, I think she may be a little homesick, though she wouldn't admit it for the world."

Then Teddi rang up Ginny Smith, and Ginny was breathless with big news. At the class meeting that afternoon Teddi had been elected chairman of the sophomore dance. "It was practically unanimous!" she said exultantly. "We don't want just a regular old party, and everybody thought you'd have a bright idea."

Through her weariness, Teddi felt a glow of pleasure. So her popularity hadn't waned completely, after all. Then the old bugaboo of time pressed down on her. "Golly, Ginny, that's awfully nice, but I don't know—"

"Don't know?" Ginny's voice rose to a peacock's shriek. "What's the matter with you, Teddi Baldwin? If you turn down this election, nobody'll ever nominate you for anything again."

Teddi knew that was probably true. She bit her lip, considered frantically, and finally managed a weak "Well, I'll try—"

"That's more like it," Ginny said with affected relief. Then she got down to business, for as vice-president of the sophomore class she took her job seriously. "You're supposed to appoint your committee and post it on the bulletin board by the end of the week. Oh, and I forgot. They decided on a date, too, this afternoon. November first. The day after Halloween."

Teddi replaced the receiver in its cradle slowly, and realized that Jane was leaning on one elbow looking at her.

"What was that all about?" she asked.

"Seems I'm to be chairman of the sophomore dance."

Jane's eyes widened respectfully. "Wow!"

But Teddi sat slumped in the telephone chair, feeling far from elated. "I don't know—" she murmured after a minute. "I'm so pushed for time—"

"Time—" Jane waved it away with an airy gesture.

"Yes, time!" Teddi said irritably. She shrugged out of her coat and went to the kitchen to discuss the situation with her mother.

Mrs. Baldwin's reaction to Teddi's election as dance chairman was much the same as Teddi's herself. "That's very nice, dear, but won't it crowd you terribly, with your dancing and all?"

"I suppose so," Teddi admitted, "but I've just got to do it." She sat down on a stool and put her head in her hands. "I couldn't play hockey on account of dancing. I can't do this and I can't do that. Everybody's going to think I'm getting peculiar if I never do *anything.* Don't you see?"

Mrs. Baldwin sympathized. "Try to get girls on your committee who will carry most of the load," she suggested. "Get everything organized quickly. Then maybe you'll make out all right."

Teddi started to work on plans for her committee right after dinner. She wrote down the subchairmen she would need—Entertainment, Decorations, Refreshment, Tickets —and decided on girls who could take responsibility.

Then there was the theme to consider. Last year's sophomore class had made it a Halloween costume affair. She couldn't repeat the scheme, but nothing novel seemed to suggest itself. Teddi fell asleep still wondering what could possibly seem original and gay. It was the next morning before she remembered to tell her mother about Justin Falk's arrival.

"Oh, and Cecile wants to know if I can come home with her for supper Wednesday night after class," Teddi added.

"They eat early, she says. I wouldn't be late. I could make the eight o'clock train."

The thought of Cecile brought with it the fact that the French girl must be getting more and more excited about the Wednesday tryouts. Cecile would never be able to understand how she—Teddi—could be dividing her interest between ballet and plans for a party. It made Teddi feel capable and a little smug.

That night, holding on to the rail at the foot of her bed, Teddi did her pliés. Then she tried a few dance steps and considered what she could see of her arabesque in the mirror over her dresser. As Madame said, it wasn't bad.

On Wednesday, Teddi was so busy at school she didn't have a chance to get scared about the tryouts. Miss Carpenter sprung an unexpected test in French class; there were the committee names to post and the members to consult about a first meeting; a guest speaker turned up at Assembly and the session was unexpectedly lengthened so that it cut into the study period during which Teddi had expected to finish her algebra. All in all, it was a full day.

But in the dressing room at Valentin's, school concerns again faded into insignificance. The girls' voices were either unexpectedly subdued or shrill with excitement. The atmosphere was as supercharged as though Justin Falk's tryouts were a professional audition. The girls were paying particular attention to their hair and clothes, concerns that worried them not in the least before an ordinary class.

"How *can* you be so nonchalant?" whispered Cecile a little wildly, as Teddi, with steady fingers, tied the ribbon that bound her ankles. Then she remembered to say, "Mother's expecting you for supper. We'll celebrate or console each other, as the case may be."

Teddi laughed and patted Cecile's shoulder. "We'll celebrate!" she insisted. "Just don't *look* frightened and you'll be all right."

But in the big practice room Teddi could feel her own

face freeze as she drew a number from a basket containing small slips of paper. Cecile's was number thirteen. Teddi's was number two.

"I'll trade you," she said.

But Cecile was superstitious. "It would be worse luck to trade number thirteen than to keep it. Anyway, I'd rather be late than early. It will give me more time to watch."

Teddi would have liked that extra time too. The knowledge that she would be the second to be called made a pulse pound in her throat. Yet she joined the group of girls waiting at the side of the room with an assumed expression of indifference. She would not let them see that their terror was epidemic. She called upon every ounce of pride she possessed.

The pianist was taking her seat as Mr. Falk strode into the room, and again Teddi was swept by self-consciousness. He was so sure, so direct, so undeniably in control of every gesture, that he made her feel like a leggy calf. All her assurance drifted away.

"You have your numbers. You'll be called in rotation. As you're called, please give me your names." Falk's voice was firm and businesslike. He stood with a foot on one of the straight chairs placed at intervals along the far wall. A pad of paper rested on his knee.

"Number one." He was wasting no time.

A short plump girl stepped forward, breathing heavily.

"I'll explain the combination," Falk said. "What's your name?"

"Phoebe Bowes," gulped the plump girl miserably, and stood in the center of the room looking as though she'd rather be dead.

"B-o-w-e-s?" asked Mr. Falk, writing on his pad. Then, when the girl only nodded, "Well? Speak up!"

The plump girl annoyed Teddi. She didn't have to act like a worm, even if she felt like one.

"Six-eight, please," came Falk's direction to the pianist.

Then he spoke to the girl. "Jeté—jeté, assemblé, brisé, entrechat, entrechat volé, back glissade, assemblé, and repeat.

"That will do," he said after a few minutes. He made a note on his pad, then called, "Next."

Teddi walked to the center of the room with her head held high. "Theodora Baldwin," she said at once, keeping her voice firm and clear to conceal her inner qualms. "Do you want me to spell it?"

Falk looked up sharply, as though he had been insulted. "No."

There was utter silence in the second before the music started. Teddi was wretchedly aware of her arms, which felt unnaturally long, like the arms of a chimpanzee she had once watched at the zoo. She knew that every eye in the room was upon her and she began to go through the steps Falk called with a bravado she was far from feeling. She forgot to smile, so intent was she on steadiness, on technique. Yet her movements had the jerkiness of a mechanical doll. She felt that she was dancing badly, yet couldn't seem to correct it. At least she was following directions without stumbling. At least on the surface she was keeping face.

Suddenly the music stopped. "Next," the dancing master was saying. It was over as quickly as that.

Teddi waited on the sidelines during the long interval before Cecile was called. She tried to watch the succession of dancers critically, and in her mind she made the choices that she thought Justin Falk might make. The dancing master's expression was inscrutable. Neither praise nor disapproval could be read in his eyes.

Cecile, whose hands had been clenched until the knuckles showed white, walked hesitantly toward the center of the floor. Her eyes looked tremendous in her pale face, and she seemed as fragile as a piece of thistledown, she was so slender and slight.

"Be good, Cecile!" Teddi implored, because she knew

how much this tryout meant to her friend.

Justin Falk looked up and for the first time he smiled. "Relax," he said with a chuckle. "I'm not an ogre."

The girls on the sidelines giggled, and a fleeting smile crossed Cecile's face. "I'll try," she said obediently, but when she began to follow his instructions she was taut as a bowstring. Only after she had been dancing for a minute or so did her usual suppleness become apparent. Then, gradually, her expression changed and she seemed to forget the instructor as she lost herself in interpreting the dance.

Falk kept her on the floor longer than the others, Teddi thought. He seemed to be watching her with special interest, and when Cecile came back to stand beside her against the barre Teddi squeezed her hand.

"He liked you," she said, and later, on the way to Cecile's apartment, Teddi was in high spirits. "You wait! When the lists are posted Friday, you'll see!" she promised. "You danced better than you ever have before."

It was fun to walk across Eighteenth Street in the gathering dusk, interesting to cross Rittenhouse Square, where old men were feeding pigeons and people were airing their dogs. Cecile lived in a third-floor apartment in a shabby house on a narrow street off Locust. The halls smelled of cooking. Spring Mill seemed very far away.

Chapter 10

Teddi came into the Baldwins' living room and threw herself on the couch. "I had the most marvelous time!" she said.

"Did you? That's nice, dear." Mrs. Baldwin, who was writing out checks at the desk, looked around and smiled. "Did you have a good dinner?"

"Mmhm." Teddi nodded dreamily. "We had little-meat."

"Little meat?"

"You say it like all one word. It's hamburger, really, but it's cooked with garlic and tomatoes and stuff and it's simply marvelous. Could we have it sometime?"

"Why, I guess so," said Mrs. Baldwin doubtfully. "If Cecile's mother could send me the recipe—"

"Oh, Mrs. Perrine says there's nothing to it," Teddi broke in with an airy wave of her hand. "You just throw in all the leftovers, and it's an awfully good way of using them up. You see, the Perrines are very economical people and they never let a scrap go to waste."

"I see," said Teddi's mother as she returned to her check-writing.

"We didn't have any dessert," Teddi vouchsafed. "The Perrines don't believe in dessert."

"Nonsense," Mr. Baldwin muttered, looking up from his newspaper.

"No, Dad, it isn't nonsense really. They're very unusual people. All they care about is art and the ballet. They don't think eating is really very important. They live on a higher plane."

"Nonsense," Mr. Baldwin repeated.

Teddi sat up, shrugged out of her coat, and addressed herself exclusively to her mother. "They know *everything* about the ballet. They used to live in New York."

"Where do they live now, Marthe?" Mr. Baldwin asked.

"Up above Rittenhouse Square," Mrs. Baldwin replied vaguely.

Mr. Baldwin asked, "How did you get to the station?"

"We walked," Teddi said. "Mrs. Perrine walked with us. Mr. Perrine was taking a nap. He has to sleep a lot because he has heart trouble." Teddi again turned to her mother. "They talk about cultural things at dinner. I think it would be nice if we did that."

Mrs. Baldwin said, "I think so too."

"You'd be surprised," Teddi went on. "They talked about Nijinsky and Danilova and Fokine as if they knew them. And Massine and Diaghileff. I think it would be marvelous to have a family like Cecile's, who really understood you. I think we live a terribly smug, middle-class existence. I think—"

"Stop thinking for a few minutes while you hang up your coat," Mr. Baldwin said irritably. "Haven't you any homework to do?"

Mrs. Baldwin shot a glance at her husband and then at her daughter, whose air of injury was great. "It is getting late, dear," she said mildly, and then, "But before you go upstairs, tell me—how did the tryouts go?"

A slight frown crossed Teddi's smooth forehead. "The list won't be posted until Friday," she said. "I don't think you can ever tell how you do *yourself.* I guess I made out all right."

"I hope so," Mrs. Baldwin said confidently.

As Teddi walked upstairs, she felt deflated. She went directly to her room, where she pulled her dress over her head, dropped her underwear to the floor, and pulled on a pair of pajamas. Then she collected the assorted rollers on which she wound her hair to give it a semblance of curl at the ends, and went into the bathroom.

Jane was stretched out in the tub, vigorously lathering soap in a futile effort to create a bubble bath effect.

"Hello," she greeted Teddi. "D'ju have fun?"

"Great fun," Teddi said without elaborating. She turned on the water, wet her comb, and began to run it through her hair.

"Guess what?" Jane said innocently, looking up. "I was elected secretary of the freshman class."

"You were?" Teddi was so surprised that she made no attempt to conceal it.

Jane wasn't offended. She nodded happily and a shy smile hovered around her lips. "I was surprised too."

"But that's neat!" Teddi recovered to say. "Congratulations, and all that stuff."

"Oh, it isn't much, really," Jane mumbled from behind the washcloth with which she was now scrubbing her face. "It's probably just because I get A's in composition and you're my sister and a secretary is supposed to be somebody who can write."

The explanation, though a little garbled, was entirely intelligible to Teddi. "It's not because you're my sister at all," she insisted magnanimously. "What you need is more self-confidence."

Jane giggled. "I'll never be like you."

"Of course you won't. You've never wanted to *be* things and *do* things desperately. You're lucky, in a way."

"I want to go away to school."

"What's the matter with Spring Mill High?"

Jane considered. "I'd like to be on my own, sort of," she said slowly. "I really would." She didn't say that Teddi had always been older and prettier and more popular, but Teddi knew that was what she meant. She had a flash of insight into the way Jane felt about herself, and she was silent and unusually thoughtful as she went back into her own room.

It was late—nearly ten o'clock—no time to be starting homework, but Teddi tossed her books on the bed, switched on the lamp on her bedside table, and made a mild effort to concentrate on her algebra problems. Figures came easily to her, as they never did to Jane. She liked the orderliness of mathematics in much the same way that she liked the precision of ballet dancing. Both were based on inviolable rules. To Teddi they made sense.

She never could understand why Jane made such a muddle of her arithmetic, why all the way through grammar school her younger sister had fretted and sweated through fractions and multiplication and long division as though they were beasts with which one must wage a bitter and losing fight.

Neat figures and symbols began to march across the paper on which Teddi worked. She checked her answers and the results pleased her. After about fifteen minutes she yawned and tucked the paper into the schoolbook, then turned out the light.

Lying in the dark, however, she didn't go to sleep at once. There was so much to think about—to wonder about. She felt ready to burst sometimes with anticipation, when, as tonight, she seemed to be living on the verge of accomplishment. There was the sophomore dance—and the plans not yet developed. There was the weekend she would spend with Pat at Miss Sinclair's. There was—overshadowing everything else—the possibility that she would, in a few days, be working with Justin Falk at Valentin's. She was both excited and terribly anxious.

There was a quality about the dancing instructor that fascinated her. His face was so alive, so mobile, his dark eyes so intense. On the surface, of course, his manner was direct and businesslike, but she was aware of a fire and a restrained power that was bound to make his dancing vivid. Every movement that he made was strong as well as graceful. She gave herself up to dreams of what it would be like to dance behind the footlights with such a partner.

Someday—someday—if she were to work very hard—

Teddi slept, and dreamed that she was actually onstage. She was the princess in *Swan Lake,* a porcelain angel in the frothiest of ballet skirts, but the danseur who was supporting her in the difficult series of lifts was not Justin Falk. It was Rod Shaw, in full football regalia, shoulder pads and all. Every time he lifted her, he grunted. It was such a silly dream that Teddi turned restlessly in bed and managed to wake herself up.

In the morning she had forgotten it, but the next time she saw Justin Falk it flashed unaccountably back into her mind. He was running up the steps at Valentin's ahead of her, and his step was youthful and springy. It was Friday, the day the list was to be posted, and as Teddi walked into the dressing room she could see a group of girls already gathered around the bulletin board. Hastily she ran over and stood on tiptoe so that she could see over Cecile's head.

Abbott, Carpenter, Corwin, Evans, Marachek, Perrine, Thomas . . .

Teddi's eyes ran down the list and for the first time a qualm of doubt smote her. She read the names again, more slowly. "Baldwin" wasn't there.

Phoebe Bowes, the fat girl who had preceded Teddi at the tryouts, turned away with a shrug. "I'm not surprised," she said to a friend. "I'd just as soon go on with Madame anyway."

But Teddi was not only surprised; she was shocked and

the emotion was written on her face for a second before she could adopt a mask of indifference. Cecile put her arm lightly across Teddi's shoulders.

"I'm awfully sorry," she whispered.

Teddi voiced the first thought that came into her head. "D'you suppose there could be some mistake?"

"I think you ought to ask Madame," Cecile said immediately. Her own elation at being included on the list was shining in her eyes but she showed a sincere concern for Teddi's plight. "You're a better dancer than half those girls he chose."

Teddi changed into her practice clothes slowly. She felt a little sick at her stomach, and her throat was tight and dry.

"Ask Madame," Cecile urged. But Lucia Valentin looked at her sympathetically and shook her head.

"I'm sorry, Teddi. I don't know myself why Mr. Falk decided against you, but that's the way it is."

Only the most determined will got Teddi through the succeeding hour. Never had her pride been so severely wounded, her mortification more complete. She was conscious that the half dozen girls chosen by Justin Falk looked at her curiously and whispered among themselves in the locker room before they sauntered into the smaller practice studio on the left of the stairs. Only Cecile's eyes showed honest sympathy, and Teddi was aware that to the rest she must have seemed arrogantly sure of herself. She even overheard one remark. "It won't hurt her to be taken down a peg."

Under Madame's tutelage, she went through her barre exercises and the subsequent centre practice disdainfully. She felt disgraced, as though she had been left behind a grade in school. She wanted to run away, to get out of the Valentin studio and stay out of it forever, yet she knew she would do no such thing. Though choking rage and resentment rose in her throat, she knew she would see this through. She wouldn't be shamed into giving up dancing, just because one teacher, however brilliant, chose to ignore her. She knew her technique was good and getting better. She'd prove it. She'd prove it to them all!

After class Teddi dressed with unprecedented speed. Falk's group hadn't returned to the locker room when she raced down the steps to the street and hurried in the direction of the station. Now, when she was alone, she could let the hot tears sting her eyelids even while her lips formed the words, "I don't care."

But she did care! She cared so much that she was weak from the sense of failure. She, Teddi Baldwin, left ignominiously behind like any clumsy dolt. She, Teddi, who had believed so firmly in a ballet career that she had given up going away to school . . .

She walked quickly, dodging in and out among the pedestrians without seeing a face she passed. With a return of a childish instinct, she wanted to get home to her mother, though she knew that this wasn't like a hurt finger that could be kissed and made all right.

She reached the station earlier than usual, entered an empty coach and sank into a seat to stare out of the window in an unhappy daze.

From wanting to get home she began to dread it. How could she confess failure to her mother? What would her father say? She was so tense that her neck began to ache. She could almost taste the humiliation that she felt. The car began to fill and the voices of people seemed harsh and obnoxiously jovial. Teddi huddled closer to the window, and her lip curled when she remembered how she had lectured Jane just two nights before on self-confidence.

"Why, Teddi Baldwin! How nice!"

Mrs. Martin, Jill's mother, sank exuberantly into the seat beside Teddi and began to arrange her packages and her pocketbook in a pyramid on her ample lap.

Teddi forced a thin smile. "Hello."

If her greeting lacked cordiality, Mrs. Martin didn't notice. "Just coming back from Valentin's, I suppose?"

Teddi nodded, wishing that Mrs. Martin were in Acapulco or Tibet.

"I do think it's so wonderful that you're studying with Valentin. You do have such talent, dear. If you only knew how my little Jill admires you. Her one ambition in life is to be able to dance like you."

At another time the woman's words, no matter how gushing, might have touched Teddi's vanity, but today she was cold to them. "I'm hardly that good," she said. "Jill has a lot to learn."

"Of course she has, dear," Mrs. Martin admitted, quite generously really, because she had misunderstood Teddi's meaning. "But she is *so* ambitious. Just like you!"

It seemed to Teddi, during the eighteen-minute ride to Spring Mill, that Mrs. Martin would never stop talking. "And I hear that this marvelous man from Hollywood has come on to teach at Valentin's. What's his name, now? Fork? Falt?"

"Justin Falk," said Teddi grimly. Yet, even as she pronounced the name, she was conscious that she felt no resentment against Mr. Falk himself for her present fall from grace. She was hurt and angry, but her contempt was turned inward. She didn't blame the dancing master for his judgment. She remembered his eyes, honest and analytical. She knew that he had tried to be fair.

"Oh, yes! Justin Falk!" Mrs. Martin was racing on. "Such a romantic name. And he looks perfectly stunning, from his newspaper picture. Is he really as good-looking as all that?"

Such a *silly* woman, Teddi was thinking. If I ever grow up to rattle on like that, I hope somebody gags me. "He's pretty good-looking," she said.

The interminable conversation dragged on. The train stopped and started, rattled along for a mile or so, then stopped at another station. Finally the conductor called "Spring Mill" and Teddi escaped to walk rapidly in the other direction from Mrs. Martin. A biting wind whipped the falling leaves and slapped at Teddi's coat. The last block she actually ran, so anxious was she to get home.

Then she opened the front door and saw Jane standing in the hallway with her face as white as paper.

"What's the matter?" The words burst forth in a gasp.

Jane's eyes were enormous and frightened as she answered. "Mother's been in an accident. They just called from the hospital," she said.

Chapter 11

Fear clutched at Teddi's heart. Accident? Hospital? She said the first words that came to her head. "Where's Dad?"

Jane seemed numb with shock. "I don't know. I called the office. He must be on his way home."

Then Teddi's questions rushed pell-mell. "Did they say what happened? Was it in the car?" She couldn't ask the most important of all—"Is she badly hurt?" She wanted to, but she couldn't get the words out.

Jane nodded. "The nurse who called said it was a collision with a truck." Her voice was scarcely above a whisper and her eyes were even wider now. Suddenly she was across the hall and had her arms around Teddi and her head on her shoulder.

"Teddi, I'm scared."

Automatically Teddi patted Jane's shoulder. She knew her sister's imagination, so much more vivid than her own, and Jane's uncontrollable trembling increased her own alarm and made her knees feel weak.

Nothing *really* bad could happen to Mother. Nothing could! If Dad would only come . . .

The sight of Flip, the puppy, suddenly racing into the hall from the kitchen carrying her favorite rubber bone, snapped Teddi's senses back to a degree of normalcy. She held Jane off by the shoulders and shook her slightly. "There's no use going to pieces. We've got to get hold of Dad and we've got to keep our heads. Now tell me *exactly.* What did the nurse say?"

"Just that. About the collision with a truck, I mean. And she said, 'Please have Mr. Baldwin get in touch with us as soon as you can reach him.' Teddi, do you think it's bad?"

"Look, Jane, there's no use wondering. We don't know. We don't know anything." To cover her sick apprehension Teddi made her voice sharp. Then she walked to the door of the living room and glanced at the shelf clock over the fireplace. "I wish Dad would come."

He was late. On this of all nights he was late.

"I'm going to call a taxi," she said abruptly. "If Dad isn't here by the time it gets here, we'll leave him a note and go to the hospital ourselves." She looked at Jane, who seemed shrunken and hunched with fear. "You write the note while I telephone. There's a pad and pencil on the desk."

Later, Teddi remembered the next ten minutes as having the slow-paced clarity of a nightmare. She walked from the living room to the hall, then back to the living room again. She opened the door, looked down the street in the direction from which her father should arrive, then came back into the house again.

Finally there was the unmistakable rattle of the taxi. "Get your coat," Teddi said to Jane.

Together, the girls went down the walk, and Teddi held open the gate while her sister went through. Then, just as the cab driver turned to open the rear door, Mr. Baldwin rounded the corner.

His hat was pushed back on his head, and he was whistling as he approached. He looked so perfectly normal and carefree that it was the hardest thing in the world for Teddi to say, "Mother's been in an automobile accident. They called from the hospital."

Mr. Baldwin didn't waste words. "Get in," he told Teddi, indicating the cab. He spoke to the driver and named the hospital. "Make it as fast as possible."

With six o'clock traffic, homebound commuters clogging the highways that spread like spokes on a wheel from the center of Philadelphia, the driver did his best. The Baldwins sat in almost complete silence after the first explanations. Jane's hand found its way under her father's arm, but Teddi sat erect and alone.

At the hospital the girls trailed behind while their father took the steps two at a time. He was already talking to the clerk at the desk when they came through the door into the big, quiet reception hall. In a second he turned and came over to them. "You wait in there," he told them gently, indicating a small room on the left of the lobby. "I'm going upstairs and I'll let you know something as soon as I can."

Teddi sank down on a leather chair and let her breath out slowly. It was so wonderful to have Dad shoulder the responsibility.

The elevators were out of sight, but she could hear the smooth opening and closing of their doors and every time they returned to the main floor she sat in tense expectation, but her father didn't come. Five minutes, ten minutes passed, and Teddi tried to smile at Jane to still her own fears.

Then, when she looked back toward the lobby, he was striding toward them across the marble floor with a vigor indicating that anxiety had been replaced by relief.

"Everything's going to be all right," he said at once. "She has a broken leg."

"A broken leg?" Jane sounded as though this were nothing to be taken lightly, but Teddi knew the news could have been much worse.

"Can we see her?" Jane asked timidly after her father had described the accident in which a truck driver, not seeing a sign at a stop street, had swerved to avoid the Baldwins' car but had nevertheless sent it glancing against a tree. "Will she come home with us?"

"You may see her," Mr. Baldwin said, "for a few minutes. But they'll keep her here tonight. After all, she's had a pretty severe shock."

Lying, small and pale, in the high hospital bed, Mrs. Baldwin smiled weakly at the girls when they came into her room. "I'm sorry I scared you all half to death," she said. "D'you suppose you can manage at home?"

"Of course we can!" Jane cried.

"We'll even remember to feed the dogs," Teddi added, trying to be cheerful, though she did think her mother looked awfully white, and there was a bandage on her temple that Dad hadn't mentioned. "You know how good Jane is at scrambling eggs."

"You're a very lucky lady!" George Baldwin said, and bent to kiss his wife. "I'll bet you look a whole lot prettier than the car."

Mrs. Baldwin shut her eyes. "The car!"

"Never mind. You're here all in one piece and that's what counts. Come on, girls!" Mr. Baldwin ordered. "We'll go get something to eat. And see that they give you a sleeping pill, Marthe. You might as well get a good night's rest."

The house, when Teddi, Jane, and their father returned to it, seemed empty and unnatural without Mrs. Baldwin, although the lights were on and the dogs were there to greet them and beg for dinner.

It was Jane, not Teddi, who now took over. She ordered her older sister around, telling her to set the table for breakfast, making sure that the alarm would go off half an hour earlier than usual, and even remembering to collect the laundry and put it in the washing machine.

"I've just been reading a book," she confessed, "where the mother and father disappear in a hurricane and the kids have to take over. There's no electricity and they haven't anything in the house to eat but some bacon and dog biscuits but they managed to have a lot of fun anyway."

"Sounds neat," said Teddi. "Which did they start gnawing on first?"

Overhearing the conversation from his chair in the living room, Mr. Baldwin relaxed and chuckled. "Look," he called, "if it's all right with you, in the morning I'll have toast with those scrambled eggs."

Teddi went to bed early. Her body ached, as though she had been beaten all over, and she didn't know that it was just reaction from protracted fear. She lay in bed, still tense, and her thoughts spun back over the exhausting day.

She could smell again the antiseptic odor of her mother's hospital room; she could see the odd bulk of the cast under the sheet. She remembered the sick hammering of her heart as she jounced along in the taxi. For the first time she realized that it must have been even worse for Jane than for her—to get the news when she was entirely alone in the house. It seemed almost ridiculous now that she could have been so shattered by Justin Falk's dismissal. It seemed unimportant, really, whether she ever danced again—at least until her mother got well.

The light was snapped off in the bathroom and Jane stood, a shadowy figure, in Teddi's bedroom door.

"You still awake?" she asked softly.

Teddi answered, "Sure."

Jane came a few steps forward. "You'll never know," she said, "how glad I was to see you when you opened that door tonight."

Teddi pushed herself up a little in bed. She couldn't see Jane's face but she could see her childish silhouette in a pair of hand-me-down pajamas.

"I can imagine!" Teddi said.

Jane sidled a little closer and sat down on the edge of the bed. "The house seems different without Mother, doesn't it?" Jane said after a minute. "Even with Dad here."

"Lonely," Teddi answered. "Is that what you mean?"
Jane nodded.

Unexpectedly, Teddi was swept by a sensation entirely new to her. She moved over in bed and threw back the covers.

"Come on. Sleep with me tonight," she suggested. "I know how you feel."

Chapter 12

Saturday morning at the Baldwins', Teddi and Jane were cleaning house. They worked from the upstairs down, taking turns with the vacuum cleaner and dustcloth, flipping a coin to see who should scrub the bathrooms, and finally ended up in the living room, where Mrs. Baldwin, her fractured leg propped up by a pillow, was talking with a visitor, Rod Shaw.

"Were you ever lucky!" he breathed. "I saw that smashed car."

"I *was* lucky," Mrs. Baldwin agreed, smiling.

"'Scuse please!" Jane, turning on the switch of the vacuum, routed Rod out of his chair.

"Here. Give me that!" he said and began to push the machine back and forth across the carpet. "Never saw a house like this. Can't give a guy a minute's peace."

Jane giggled. "You sound just like Dad." Then she examined the section of rug he had just abandoned. "Look at these dog hairs. You'd better come back over this."

Teddi, who was waxing the pine mantel, turned around. "I wish you'd all try to think of something original we might do for the sophomore dance." She looked genuinely concerned.

"I'll tell you something awfully original," said Rod. "Invite the whole class here and have a housecleaning bee."

"What's the date of this party?" Mrs. Baldwin asked.

"The day after Halloween. But a Halloween dance is just too obvious. Anyway, that was done last year."

"How about a barn dance?" Rod said. "It's fall."

"A barn dance isn't very *different*," Teddi said slowly.

"It could be," Mrs. Baldwin suggested thoughtfully from the couch. "You could have an old-fashioned square dance and all come in country calicos and farm togs."

"Oh, Mother, the kids don't want to spend the evening square dancing. That's something we do in gym."

Mrs. Baldwin was undaunted. "There used to be a wonderful old caller who lived up Beaver Hollow way. He played the fiddle like a real pro. *There* you'd have something different—if you could get him!"

"Say!" said Rod, and even Teddi began to look interested.

"Do you think the boys would go along with it?" she asked.

"I don't see why not. They're just naturally balky at the beginning of a party any way you look at it. An old-fashioned fiddler might shake them loose."

"Would he be expensive?" Teddi began to wonder.

"I don't think so," her mother replied.

"Raise the price of the tickets," Rod said airily. "The sophomores are rich."

"That's more than you can say for the freshmen," Jane groaned. "You ought to see our treasurer's report."

Suddenly Rod glanced at the clock. "Yipe!" he said in alarm. "I've got to get out of here." He dropped the vacuum handle and grabbed his jacket as he made for the door. "If you want to look up that old fiddler, I'll borrow Dad's car and drive you up-country," he called to Teddi over his shoulder. Then he was gone.

Jane offered generously to finish up the kitchen, and

Teddi held her meeting in the living room, where her mother could act in an advisory capacity if needed. Tactfully, Teddi asked for suggestions before she made any proposal, no matter how tentative, of her own. Her committee—as Mrs. Baldwin put it later—was longer on looks than on creative ideas, and after ten minutes of fruitless conversation Teddi said casually, "Rod Shaw was just here. He suggested a barn dance."

"But a barn dance isn't anything unusual," the ticket chairman complained, though not without a trace of respect for Rod.

"Boys don't like parties that are *too* unusual," Teddi said. She described the idea for costumes and for square dancing, intimating that these were Rod's suggestions too. It wasn't until Mrs. Baldwin described how amusing a fiddling caller would be that the girls began to get a sparkle of interest in their eyes.

Of course the question of whether the boys would cooperate in even a minimum number of square dances had to be discussed at length, but finally, for want of an alternate proposal, Teddi's plan won.

"Now I hope we'll find that old Billy Timpkins, the fiddler, is still alive," murmured Mrs. Baldwin when the girls had left.

Teddi collapsed in the wing chair. "Don't even *think* anything else," she cautioned superstitiously.

Out in the kitchen Teddi could hear her father dump a box of groceries on the table. She heaved herself out of the chair with a sigh. Ever since her mother had been incapacitated, Teddi hadn't had many minutes when she could just sit.

Concern flashed across Mrs. Baldwin's face. "I'm sorry—" she began.

Passing the couch, Teddi impulsively bent and kissed the top of her head. "I'm not tired," she denied. "I was just sighing on general principles. You go to sleep for half an hour and when you wake up we'll have lunch."

Meal-getting was now a cooperative affair. Mr. Baldwin and the girls each had their special duties, and they laughed a lot while they were working. Never before had Teddi realized that Dad, who usually came home from the office and plopped down in a chair with a newspaper, could be so much fun.

Jane, however, was the real organizer of the three. It was she who actually managed to get meals on the table that were edible and hot. It was she who thought up menu ideas that would be simple but not repetitive.

Teddi was more surprised than her dad at Jane's unexpected ability. She felt incompetent and slow by comparison, but she was determined to do her share. Yesterday, she had called Valentin's to report her mother's accident and tell Madame's secretary that she would have to cancel her lessons for a few weeks. She knew it might seem to some of her classmates that she had taken offense at Justin Falk's decision against her, but she had to take the chance of appearing petty. She couldn't let Jane shoulder all the responsibility at home.

After lunch Teddi called Rod. "Still game to drive me to Beaver Hollow?" she asked.

"Sure. How about tomorrow afternoon?"

For the first time since their quarrel on the night of the ballet, Teddi was alone with Rod, and though this couldn't be called an actual date she still felt that it was a step toward the reestablishment of their former cordial relations.

"Beaver Hollow or Bust!" she dubbed their expedition at the outset, and after some of the rough roads they drove over to reach the little hamlet, Rod said he thought it should just be called "Bust."

But the car managed to withstand the jouncing of the country ruts, and they arrived, finally, at a general store and gas station on the ridge above a cuplike valley. The proprietor pointed out a little house in the hollow. "Old Bill, he lives down there. But you're likely not to find him at home. He's apt to be at his daughter's, over Chadd's Ford way, or out settin' muskrat traps along Tumble Creek, or even down at the firehouse in the village, just settin' in the sun. You never can tell."

"We'll try the house first," decided Rod. "But in case he isn't there, could you tell us his daughter's name?"

The store owner scratched his head. "'Twas Timpkins, of course," he allowed, "but now seems like it's Miller, or Millbank, or maybe Marshall. Can't say as I recollect for sure."

Rod thanked the man, and Teddi joined in rather dubiously. "Maybe we should have brought our pajamas and toothbrushes," Teddi said as they started down the steep hill. "This looks like an all-night job."

But to their amazement, before the door of the ramshackle little house in the valley sat a skinny, old fellow with thick white eyebrows and blue eyes as bright as a boy's. He stopped tinkering with a pile of muskrat traps and looked up at them quizzically.

"Are you Mr. Timpkins?" Teddi asked.

"None other," he admitted, "but call me Billy. Seems less formal-like. Ain't heard the mister in years."

Teddi explained why they had come. "To tell the truth, we're not sure we can afford you," she ended. "How much do you charge?"

"How much have you got?"

"Forty dollars," Teddi replied. "You see, it's a class party, and we're only sophomores—"

"Could you stretch it to fifty?"

"Nope," Rod broke in, "but we'll come get you and bring you back. That's fair enough."

Old Billy looked from the boy to the girl, then grinned, deciding to capitulate. "It's a deal."

During the next week notices began to appear on homeroom bulletin boards, in the school paper, even scrawled on the blackboards of the chemistry laboratory. They were provocative and brief.

> "Chassez right across the hall—
> Chassez back and kick that ball!"
> You'll get your chance at the Sophomores'
> HARVEST HOEDOWN
> Spring Mill High School Gymnasium
> NOVEMBER 1

Or again would appear this advice—

> "Come as your Great Aunt Min or
> Uncle Ephraim to the Harvest Hoedown,"

and Teddi would be deluged by questions galore.

> "Ever been a first top lady?
> You'll get your chance, gals, at the
> Harvest Hoedown!"

Again came a suggestion scrawled in chalk.

> "You're going wrong, the other way.
> You should be headed for the Sophomores'
> Harvest Hoedown."

Only Rod Shaw and Teddi knew that Mrs. Baldwin had thought up the advertising stunt.

Chapter 13

To go back to classes at Valentin's after a three-week absence was something that took every bit of courage and determination that Teddi Baldwin possessed.

To go back as Justin Falk's pupil would have been thrilling, even though she might have fallen behind the rest of the class. But to go back to study with the second section under Madame, to practice along with clumsy creatures like Phoebe Bowes, who had no more chance of becoming a ballerina than Sherry—that, for Teddi, was really eating crow.

At times, she didn't know why she returned at all. With cameo clearness she remembered her mother's request on the great day of her reprieve from Miss Sinclair's.

"If you find your dancing isn't living up to your expectations, tell me, Teddi. If you're losing interest in it, tell me that too."

Teddi remembered how sure she had been that to go on with her dancing could never be a mistake.

If only wishing could make things so! In her desire to be a ballerina, Teddi hadn't changed, but her belief in her own ability was shaken, shaken so severely that she hadn't told anyone—not even her mother—that she had failed to win inclusion among Justin Falk's group.

Teddi was a little ashamed that she hadn't told. She felt, in a way, that she was not keeping faith. On that first evening of heartbreak she could have flung herself into her mother's arms and sobbed out the miserable story of failure, but the accident had torn her own predicament from Teddi's mind, and afterward there had never come an appropriate time. Nor could she bear to admit that she was considered second-rate. Teddi Baldwin had always been better than average, often been best. If she had to pull herself up by the straps of her own ballet shoes, she would climb to that position again!

So with her chin in the air she faced the music. Three afternoons a week, sweating at the barre, repeating the heel and knee stretches, backbends and splits, Teddi worked as she had never worked before.

Madame was not unappreciative. "Perhaps all of my pupils should take a vacation," she said. "Yours has been good for your dancing. It is a strange thing."

It was a little strange even to Teddi. When she might understandably have felt crushed by disappointment and failure, she knew that she was dancing with more vitality and expression than ever before.

In an unformed way she felt that this had something to do with her mother's accident and the warm sense of family loyalty it had engendered. Yet how such a thing could have any bearing on the correct execution of relevé turns in second . . . ?

Meanwhile, life was racing along at such a clip that she didn't have much time to dwell on psychological causes and effects. The Harvest Hoedown was only a week away, and there were a thousand and one last-minute arrangements about which every member of her committee consulted Teddi. Being the chairman of the big sophomore dance of the year was no part-time job.

At night, when she got back from dancing class, half a

dozen telephone messages would await her, noted down in Jane's round, careful hand. Everybody in the family tried to ease her lot, yet they couldn't give her the one thing she most needed—more time.

Mrs. Baldwin was now limping around the kitchen in a walking cast. Her family was ecstatic over her cooking, appreciating for the first time its superiority to their own best efforts. After dinner each evening Teddi helped Jane clean up; then there was homework, more telephone calls, and eventually bed.

She was asleep, each night, two minutes after her head touched the pillow. She didn't yet have a date for the dance, but she was too tired to be much concerned.

About one thing she was delighted. Her mother had made her a costume—an ankle-length skirt of peasant fullness, the same ripe wheat color as Teddi's hair, and with it a blouse of white batiste that had huge puff sleeves. It was pretty enough for a summer dress when its present use was past, and the green and red braid banding the skirt gave it just the right country fillip.

"You look like a cross between a Scandinavian peasant and a musical comedy queen," her father teased when she tried it on.

"I'm the young girl in *The Blue Danube*," Teddi told him airily. And she kicked off her sneakers and did a few experimental ballet steps.

Jane watched her deferentially for a few minutes, then leaned against her mother and sighed. "Golly, wouldn't you think I'd have been born with some talent?" she asked.

Mrs. Baldwin laughed and put her arm around Jane's shoulders. "You have one of the greatest talents of all; you make people love you," she said.

Teddi stopped dancing abruptly and cocked her head to one side. That's right, she was thinking. It was a remark she wouldn't have understood a few weeks before, when she had considered Jane just a rather tiresome child, but now she was beginning to recognize her sister's essential quality.

Glancing at Teddi and then at each other, Mr. and Mrs. Baldwin began to laugh because she looked so surprised, but Jane buried her head in her mother's shoulder, flushed and embarrassed. "You're teasing me." It was impossible for Jane to believe anything really flattering about herself.

It was typical, when school closed at two thirty for a special teachers' meeting the next day, that Teddi should catch an earlier train to town than usual and take advantage of the extra time to work alone in the empty practice room at Valentin's. She loaded the record player, and after spending ten minutes at the barre she went over in front of the huge mirror that covered half of one wall and, watching her image critically, she practiced her fouettés.

After a few minutes, because she was alone and because the music was tempting, she began to improvise. She tried some relevés arabesques and, after a while, she forgot to watch herself in the glass and danced as she sometimes did when there was no one in the house at home, for the sheer love of dancing. She only stopped when the record stopped, breaking off without self-consciousness and walking toward the phonograph to start the music again.

"Where have you been?"

A voice filled with lively curiosity made Teddi whirl around. Then, in spite of herself, she flushed scarlet. Justin Falk was standing in the studio door.

"What do you mean where have *I* been?" Teddi was abashed, yet her voice held a faint note of truculence. She met Falk's eyes.

"You didn't dance like that a month ago," the young man said. "You danced then like a mechanical doll."

Teddi's chin began to go up in the air defensively, and without warning Justin Falk began to laugh. He laughed wholeheartedly, his eyes crinkling at the corners and his narrow head thrown back. He wasn't ridiculing her; he was just frankly amused.

Teddi's defense crumbled with his next words. "Don't be angry. I'm trying to pay you a compliment. Today you danced with warmth"—he paused, seeking a more exact adjective—"with heart."

Before the surprise of such an appraisal, Teddi dropped her eyes. Then, with a change of mood which was typical of the dancing instructor, Falk became businesslike.

"Try those relevés arabesques again," he ordered, and stood back against the big mirror, his legs crossed nonchalantly, watching her.

Teddi, nervous and self-conscious now, did her best.

"No, no, no!" Falk interrupted before she had finished. "Like this!" He showed her expertly. "See?"

Teddi nodded, and tried again. This time it was she who shook her head. Then she tried a third time, and Falk said, "That's better."

He worked with her for fifteen minutes, until the first of the girls in Teddi's class began to saunter in from the locker room to take their places at the barre. Then he glanced at the wall clock, and said abruptly, "Go in and join my group today. I'll speak to Madame." Without another glance in her direction, he turned and walked out of the room.

Teddi wasn't sure what the invitation meant as she stood looking after him. It could be a permanent promotion, or it could be for only this afternoon. She walked back to the locker room to whisper the news to Cecile, but she didn't want to count on anything until she was sure.

Cecile, however, squeezed Teddi's arm in delight. "I *knew* if he could see you dance again, he'd realize!"

But Teddi shook her head at the inference that Mr. Falk had made a mistake. "He didn't like my dancing then. He just thinks I've gotten better."

During the next hour Teddi worked with such great intensity of purpose that she was only dimly aware that there were other girls dancing beside her, going through the same exercises and the same steps. Only Justin Falk, of all the people in the room, seemed real, and under the command of his personality she concentrated on striving for the freedom that is every ballerina's ideal.

The sixty minutes slipped by like a second, and before Teddi knew it she was again sitting on the dressing room bench next to Cecile, mopping her perspiring forehead and wriggling her bare toes.

"Isn't he marvelous?" she sighed.

Cecile nodded. "He can dance as well as he can teach, too. I guess it's because he's so young. There aren't many ballet masters like that."

Teddi looked at Cecile curiously. There was thoughtfulness and appreciation in her eyes, but not the special glow that shone in Teddi's. Cecile could be critical; she could stand off and consider. She hadn't caught fire, as Teddi had. For her, Justin Falk was simply a superior teacher; he wasn't a dynamic force, a compelling personality, a man.

But in a single afternoon Teddi's whole world had changed. As she walked to the station from the studio she felt lighter than air, able to float along the pavement, and when she thought of Justin Falk she saw him leaning with supreme nonchalance against the huge mirror, and a little chill chased up her spine. She felt as though she hugged to herself a wonderful secret, but she didn't know quite what the secret was. The Harvest Hoedown, school, home—all seemed evanescent. Only Justin Falk—Justin Falk and her dancing—were substantial and alive in her mind.

On the train she got a seat by the window; she sat with her feet warmed by the piping, her chin in her hand. A large, tired woman with arms full of department store purchases edged in next to her and Teddi shrank still farther within herself, keeping her head turned toward the window. She felt full of an expandable, physical vigor that threatened to engulf her.

Of course, at home, none of the other Baldwins knew. Mrs. Baldwin greeted her with, "Teddi, Flip has just chewed a hole in the elbow of your blue sweater. Why *will* you persist in leaving your clothes scattered all over the floor?"

Jane said, "Teddi, Rod just telephoned," as though it were a message of great importance. "He said he'd call back."

Mr. Baldwin said, "Now that Teddi's home, let's eat. I'm starved."

And all the time Teddi, who felt ready to burst, acted no differently than she had on a hundred previous nights. She helped carry serving dishes to the table as though nothing had happened at all.

Chapter 14

A Halloween moon, bright and round as an orange ball, hung in the sky on the night of the Harvest Hoedown. Teddi leaned out of her bedroom window to inspect it more closely, and Jane, who lay sprawled across the bed watching her sister dress, asked, "What time's Rod coming?"

"Early. We're going to have to go all the way up to Beaver Hollow to get Billy Timpkins. But now that we know the way maybe it won't seem so far."

Teddi gave her shining hair a last brush, lifting it from her shoulders and enjoying the scratching of the bristles along the nape of her neck. She looked lovely and she knew it. The basque emphasized the creaminess of her skin, so close to the color of her hair. She felt again the thrill of excitement that had possessed her at intervals ever since the afternoon of her discovery by Justin Falk.

"Aren't you glad you're going with Rod?" Jane asked without looking directly at Teddi, then rolled over on her back and began to hum an indistinct tune.

"Sure," Teddi replied, forgetting how awkward the lack of Rod's escort would have made things. "Sure."

Repeated, the word carried more conviction. She *was* glad that she was going with Rod. He was a nice boy, sort of like a pleasant older brother, homey and competent and substantial, but he wasn't anybody to get especially breathless over. He couldn't be compared to somebody like Justin Falk.

"I think it was pretty decent of Rod to ask you—after the way you've treated him."

"The way I've treated him?" Teddi paused. "What do you mean?"

Jane squirmed, as though she had already said too much. Then she bounced off the bed and went over to switch on the table radio. "Oh, I don't know."

Dance music, lingering and sweet, didn't drown the sharp clack of the front door knocker. Teddi put down her brush and stepped back for a final inspection.

"You'll do." Jane grinned with a sudden change of mood.

"Teddi! It's Rod."

"All right, Mother. Thank you!"

Teddi turned to Jane. "You going down? Tell him I'm getting my coat."

But Jane shrank into herself abruptly. Her hands flew to her hair and her eyes to the mirror. "I can't go down looking like this!"

Teddi, opening the closet door, shrugged and laughed lightly. "You're a changed creature these days, Janey. What's got into you?"

Rod was impatient to be off. He had on an open-necked plaid flannel shirt, jeans, and a tattered straw hat pushed far back on his head. As Teddi ran down the stairs he whistled appreciatively, then glanced at his wristwatch. "We've got to hurry."

Old Billy, fortunately, didn't keep them waiting. He was sitting in front of the general store when they arrived at the top of the Beaver Hollow hill and he flagged them down by waving a battered fiddle case.

The first of the sophomores were just beginning to straggle into the gym when Teddi and Rod got back to Spring Mill with their companion. In his rusty brown coat and yellow checked shirt Mr. Timpkins fitted into the Harvest Hoedown picture like a hand into a glove. His rheumy eyes twinkled and his mouth quirked upward in a smile. The minute he saw the gym floor, he tested it with his foot appreciatively.

"Got a fine place here," he said.

The gym did look marvelous, Teddi remarked with pride. The decorating committee must have gathered in the sheaves from a good many neighboring farms. Corn shocks were stacked in the corners, a country post lamp was rigged up by the door, and the windowsills were bright with apples and pumpkins arranged in careless, decorative heaps.

From the basket at one end of the ball court hung a harvest moon just as fabulous and round as the one that actually adorned the night. A buggy and a straw-filled comic horse were hitched to a bar of the climbing ladder, and it was here that Teddi planned to have Mr. Timpkins stand. Then he would have a place to sit during the intervals in which there was no square dancing, and he would be safely out of the melee on the floor.

All the qualms that Teddi had previously felt as to the success of her plan had deserted her. As a matter of fact, in the past week, she realized that her attitude had completely changed toward the dance and toward Rod, too. She had been pleased when he had called to ask her to go with him, but not overjoyed. It was as though she were living in a rather pleasant dream, as though all the home and school things were arranging themselves in patterns without any help from her. She felt no urgency, no special anxiety, nor pride in achievement. She smiled at everyone, liked everyone, but at the same time she pitied them, rather, because they couldn't know how thrilling and marvelous life could be—studying ballet under Justin Falk.

Rod said, "D'you think that buggy's going to hold him?

Looks kind of creaky to me."

Teddi replied, "Mr. Timpkins isn't a heavy man. If he doesn't like it, he can climb down."

But old Billy was enthralled with his perch. He opened his fiddle case and tuned up, then sat beaming on the buggy seat while Teddi brought the members of her committee over to be introduced.

Rod, now that the night was here, was especially solicitous, because of the part he had played in developing the party idea.

"If the boys herd up and hang around the record player all evening, I'll beat their heads in," he threatened in an undertone, glancing at the inevitable group of misogynists.

"You do that!" Teddi encouraged him. "But give them a chance to get into the swing of things first."

As Teddi had expected, the first square dance to be called was really an exhibition number, with only two teachers and the committee members and their escorts participating. The rest of the sophomores stood on the sidelines, looking a little dubious, although old Billy's fiddle had their feet tapping.

"Salute your partners, corners all, and it's eight hands around!" The directions were so easy to follow, and the figures were so familiar to the girls from gym class, that the dancers began to forget themselves, and by the time the fiddler shouted "Swing your partners!" they were laughing out loud.

The hilarity, like old Billy's music, was contagious. The next dance Teddi started off as a Paul Jones, then Mr. Timpkins blew a whistle and announced that the present partners would form sets for "Pop Goes the Weasel." A few couples, shy or suspicious, dropped out, but the gym floor was filled with ducking, swinging "gents" and "ladies" who even sang their own refrain:

"And that's the way your money goes,
Pop goes the weasel!"

Old Billy was standing with one foot on the buggy seat now, tapping out the rhythm with his toe as he played. The singing tickled him so much that he forgot the record player was to take its turn.

"Let's do 'Buffalo Gals'!" he called out, and began to play the tune of "Camptown Races," then climbed down from his perch to illustrate the way the dance should go.

Before long he had new sets organized, and in five minutes the sophomore boys were whooping like Indians, "Aha-ha-ha and aho-ho-ho!"

Even the members of Teddi's committee began to relax. The command performance was over, the smiles were genuine rather than determined, the Harvest Hoedown was on the road to success.

Teddi accepted her position as belle of the ball gracefully. In the intervals between the square dances, she was never without a partner. When she wasn't dancing with Rod she was claimed by one of the other boys, and she smiled at all of them.

Her detachment reacted in a curious way on the boys in her crowd. They made an extra effort when they were with her. Although her attitude baffled them, it also intrigued them. Teddi Baldwin became not only a pretty but an interesting and rather glamorous girl.

Not being given to self-analysis, Teddi could not account for her own feeling of being suspended a little above the happenings of the moment. She was glad things were going well, but not ecstatic. She recognized the flavor of popularity, yet it wasn't uncommonly sweet.

Only once during the evening was she swept by any strong emotion. Mr. Harwood, the math teacher, had courteously asked her to be his partner in a square dance, and Teddi had of course accepted. He was a heavy man, soon breathing rapidly from the exercise, but he had learned the figures old Billy called during summer vacations in a New England village where traditional dancing was the Saturday night diversion. There was an expertness in the way he swung her in place, a man's strength about him, that made Teddi think of Justin Falk.

For a split second she closed her eyes. Falk, not fat Mr. Harwood, was her partner. A tremulous excitement swept her and a tingling sensation ran across her shoulders and down her arms.

"Tired?" Mr. Harwood asked.

"Oh, no!" Teddi smiled sweetly, and Mr. Harwood decided she was an unusually attractive girl.

"You've put on a nice dance," he said. "You're to be congratulated."

"Thank you," Teddi replied. The short spell was broken. She began to look around with mild interest for Rod.

Chapter 15

Teddi's weekend with Pat Rutherford at Miss Sinclair's followed hard on the heels of the Harvest Hoedown.

"Do I *have* to go?" Teddi asked her mother a few days before the date set. She was so increasingly absorbed by her dancing that the trip, in anticipation, seemed more of an effort than a pleasure.

Jane, listening to the conversation, held her head with both hands. "Does she *have* to go! Why don't you tell Pat to ask me?"

Mrs. Baldwin looked at Teddi with a small frown of concern. "I think it will do you good. You look thin."

Jane giggled. "Do you expect one weekend of boarding school food to fatten her up?"

Mrs. Baldwin pursued her own train of thought. "It's this dancing; it's like an obsession—"

"Mother, anybody who gets anywhere works hard!"

Mrs. Baldwin looked at her daughter intently. She sighed and said, "Yes, I suppose you're right."

Three days later Teddi found herself on a westbound bus. Her bag was on the rack above her head, and beside it was a box of food packed for Pat by Mrs. Rutherford. Jane had nodded at the box approvingly. "You can have a midnight feast," she said.

With the soothing sound of the bus wheels beneath her, and the pleasant sensation of being safely started on a journey, Teddi began to relax. She wondered whether Pat would have changed. They had always been such fast friends, sharing each other's secrets, discussing each other's ambitions and disappointments. She hoped she would still be able to really *talk* to Pat.

Somehow, in the few short months since school had started, Teddi felt so much older. She sat staring out the window at the brown November fields and wondered what had given her this sense of change—her mother's accident, her new feeling of family responsibility, her growing and rather unexpected affection for Jane, or the coming of Justin Falk?

In Summerton, where Miss Sinclair's school was located on the edge of the village tucked between rolling Pennsylvania hills, Pat was waiting impatiently. She ran to Teddi and grabbed her overnight bag. "I was *so* afraid something would go wrong!"

"Don't crush this box!" Teddi warned. "It's full of goodies for a midnight feast."

"Full of what?"

"That's Jane's version," Teddi told her. "You know Jane and her boarding school books."

They both laughed, and any sense of strain that might have arisen with the meeting disappeared. Side by side they walked to the taxi stand, and suddenly there was so much to talk about that neither of them knew where to begin.

Pat, Teddi thought, looked marvelous. She had let her hair grow until it was almost waist length, and it was brushed and shining. Her eyes had never seemed so bright, nor her color so high, and even her walk had a new assurance. Going away to school had apparently been just the thing for Pat.

Riding through the little village in the taxi, Teddi realized for the first time how much she had missed Pat. None of the other girls quite took Pat's place; there was no one else in whom she ever felt the right to confide.

At the moment, Pat was busy being the anxious hostess. "I think you'll love the school," she said. "Even if some of the girls pretend that it's dismal, I love it just the same. And literally *every*body is dying to meet you, Teddi. I've told them all about you—about your dancing and everything—"

"Oh, Pat, you shouldn't have!" Teddi could imagine Pat's buildup. It made her feel self-conscious and alarmed. A small frown of irritation drew her brows downward until Pat turned troubled eyes on her.

"But—"

Teddi smiled, in spite of herself. "You dope."

It was always that way. She could never get really mad at Pat. Pat was too much like Flip or Sherry—too loyal and sweet and affectionate—to incur any permanent ire.

"They'll adore you," Pat insisted, still talking about her schoolmates. "And you'll like them. Particularly Mary Lou."

Who Mary Lou might be Teddi had to wait to discover. The cab was turning into a curving drive between two stone pillars which supported a wrought iron gate. Teddi could catch a glimpse of some low-lying buildings of a mellow red brick, half covered with ivy.

"You should have seen this place in October." With newfound loyalty Pat sang its praise. "There's the gym, and that's the dormitory, and Miss Sinclair lived here."

Teddi's head kept twisting from side to side until the cab pulled up at a flight of steps. It seemed strange to think of Pat living in this atmosphere, when all her life she'd eaten and slept and studied in the old Rutherford house on Glen Road. It also seemed somewhat disturbing that she no longer knew everything about Pat's life.

Within, the building they entered was far less impressive than on the outside, where the wandering ivy softened signs of age. The stairs up which Teddi followed Pat were worn with the hurrying feet of successive generations of girls, and there were cracks in the plaster which not even diligent repainting could hide.

It occurred to Teddi that it must have looked much the same when her mother was a pupil here, and the shabbiness became more interesting because of this. She should have asked her mother which room she'd had, because, by pure coincidence, Pat might now have the same one.

"Do you have a roommate?" Teddi asked.

Pat shook her head. "Mother thought it would be better for me to be alone, because you know what I'm like. I'd never get any studying done."

From behind closed doors came the sound of girls' voices, of laughter. A shower was running somewhere and the bather was singing, filling in when she didn't know the words of a popular song with an unconcerned "dum-dum-dum." A terry cloth-robed figure scooted across the hall ahead of Pat and Teddi, and a radio was twisted from station to station by an unseen hand. Teddi had never been in a preparatory school before and it all seemed different and therefore fascinating.

"Here's where I live," Pat said.

She pushed a door open on a plaster-walled cubicle with a table-desk, an easy chair, and the usual couch-type bed on which a red-haired girl was lying on her back, casually filing her nails.

The girl sat up when she saw Pat, and her gray-green eyes took in Teddi at a glance. "Hi." Her voice made the monosyllable soft.

"Hi!" Pat sounded pleased. She introduced Teddi, saying, "This is Mary Lou Blake I've been telling you about."

Teddi could see that Mary Lou was older, and she also

seemed more sophisticated than any of the girls in Spring Mill.

"I came up to see if you have any decent nail polish," Mary Lou said after she had greeted Teddi offhandedly. "I'm going to the Academy dance tonight..." Her explanation faded perfectly logically into thin air.

"I'll see." Pat started to root through the top drawer of the bureau. Meanwhile Mary Lou turned to Teddi.

"You're the dancer," she said more in assertion than inquiry. "Isn't that *interesting.*"

Instead of feeling interesting Teddi suddenly felt tongue-tied and gauche. Mary Lou's tone dismissed dancing as something one would only consider as a last resort, if everything else—including Miss Sinclair's School—failed.

"She's marvelous!" Pat insisted, her back to them both. "I've told you!"

Teddi recovered some of her poise. "Pat always brags about her friends," she laughed. "And if she likes a person, she always thinks they're pretty."

Mary Lou looked at Teddi sharply for an instant, and Teddi realized that she had scored with no malicious intent. Because Mary Lou really was pretty, with dark eyelashes and burnt-orange hair. She had a languorous kitten look, and a studied way of using her eyes and hands that annoyed Teddi as much as it apparently intrigued Pat.

Teddi was glad when she left, bearing the nail polish, yet the minute the door was closed she had to ask Pat more about Mary Lou. How old was she? Where did she live? What was she really like?

"She's wonderful!" Pat said at once. "She's a junior this year, but she's really a little old for her class, because her mother took her to Europe and she missed two years in school when she was a child."

Teddi had taken off her coat and shoes and was wriggling her toes, sitting on Pat's bed with her knees under her chin and her arms around her legs.

"Did you ever *see* such a complexion?" Pat enthused. "She uses buttermilk soap all the time and her mother—she used to be an actress—sends her the most luscious creams. She says I can get rid of my freckles if I use lemon juice every night—I started but somehow I keep forgetting. What's the matter, Teddi?"

"Your freckles are all right," Teddi retorted in a rather testy voice. Then, to change the subject, she added, "You've gotten thin, Pat."

Pat turned around on one heel. "Didn't I tell you school food would do it?"

The mention of food reminded Pat of her mother's box, but the lunch bell rang before she had the string untied. "Saturday lunch is terrible," she said, "but we might as well show up and you can meet the kids at my table—the ones that aren't away for the weekend. And afterward we'll bring some of them back here for food."

Teddi, lacking Pat's exposure to the monotony of institutional cooking, didn't think lunch was bad at all. And she was interested in the girls she met, though she had a hard time remembering their names. The thin one with glasses and bangs was Brick, and the fat one with the deep voice was Suzy, but who the straight-haired brown one and the china-doll blonde were Teddi never did get straight. At any rate they all came back to Pat's room after lunch and ate Mrs. Rutherford's fresh fruit and brownies with squeals of appreciation. But for the fact that it's noon instead of midnight, Teddi decided, Jane wasn't so far wrong.

It was apparent, as the weekend progressed, that Pat was well liked. Teddi was impressed by her success in an environment to which she was a stranger. She had developed poise; she was more graceful in her manner; she had lost that childish habit of ducking her head when she was embarrassed; she was more of a person in every respect except one.

And that one was her patent adoration of Mary Lou Blake. She began talking about her again when they were swimming in the gym pool later in the afternoon.

"You ought to see Mary Lou do a swan dive. It's really something!" And later—"Mary Lou lives in New York, and her mother teaches dramatic art. Maybe that's why she seems so different from all the girls at home."

Teddi grunted, turned a somersault in the water, then came up and said, "I think she seems affected, sometimes."

"Oh, but she's not, really. If you could see her mother, you'd realize! They're marvelous together. Not like anyone I've ever met."

Pat's enthusiasm was so genuine that Teddi, in a curious way, did begin to understand. Justin Falk was like that, utterly different, so far removed from common clay that it seemed right to idolize him. She wondered if she could tell Pat about Justin Falk.

Once the idea had occurred to her, Teddi couldn't resist the urge to confide in Pat. That night, when the lights were out and she was snuggled under the covers of the folding cot that had been moved for the occasion into Pat's room, she lay tense with excitement and after a while she raised herself on one elbow and said, "Pat—"

Pat turned over on her stomach and propped her chin in her hands. "Mmmm?"

"Pat, did you ever feel that the boys we know were sort of—well, Mother has a word for it—callow?"

Pat considered. "Not especially. Why?"

"Well, I mean when you meet somebody—older, it seems as if they laugh too loud and cut up too much, and sort of jerk themselves around. Oh, I don't know—"

Pat laughed. "Sure, but they'll get over it, in time. By the way, how's Rod?"

Teddi waved a hand, vaguely. "Oh Rod—" She sighed, then said, "He's all right. He took me to the sophomore dance. I was chairman." Disinterestedly, she left her voice trail off.

"You were? That's great."

"It was all right," Teddi said, "but it took up an awful lot of time, and with my dancing—" She let the sentence die, then rushed on. "Did I tell you I have a new ballet teacher?"

"Huh-uh." Pat yawned.

"He's from Hollywood," Teddi said. "His name is Justin Falk, and he's a perfectly marvelous dancer!"

"You and your dancing!" Pat said.

But Teddi scarcely heard her. She wriggled to a sitting position and hugged her knees tight with her arms.

"You've never seen anything like his eyes, and he has hair that fits his head like a cap, and he's young, Pat. At least he's not old. He's maybe"—Teddi took a wild guess—"well, twenty-five."

Pat turned over and pushed the pillow into a hard knob under her neck. "Twenty-five? What do you mean he's not old?"

But Teddi couldn't be deterred. "You'd understand if you could see him, honestly you would."

Pat turned on her side and propped her cheek with her hand. "Maybe I would," she said slowly. "Mary Lou says it's very broadening for a girl to fall in love with an older man."

In the darkness Teddi flushed crimson. "Oh, it isn't that way, Pat. Good grief, Justin Falk never even looks at me!"

Chapter 16

For Teddi the interval between Thanksgiving and midyear whisked by with the speed of one of the jet planes that passed overhead.

Christmas was always a breathless, happy time, and this year it seemed even more exciting and beautiful than ever, with its carol-singing and its tree-trimming and its warming sense of family friendship.

It was during Christmas vacation that Jane had her first real date. She went to a private party with Tommy Scott, a boy from her class. At the last minute she wailed, "Teddi, what am I ever going to *talk* about?"

"Don't talk too much. Just look as if you were glad to be with him. Remember, he'll be scared too. And if you do talk, make it about something Tommy's interested in. That's all there is to it, really, Jane."

She told her mother about the conversation after Jane had left, and admitted, "I remember that awful tongue-tied feeling. But she'll get over it. Jane's O.K."

Teddi had further cause to remember that tongue-tied feeling a month later, because it swept over her again one afternoon when she was sitting in the drugstore next to the Valentin studio having a chocolate milk shake, and getting over it wasn't as easy as she had led Jane to believe.

Midyear examinations had started and Teddi had finished her French written exam early and caught an express to town. Hunger gnawed at her stomach in a typical after-exam manner and she decided she simply had to have something to eat before she could possibly practice.

She was just pushing the straws out of their paper envelope when a voice next to her said, "What's that?" and she turned to look straight into the eyes of Justin Falk.

"A-a milk shake." Teddi considered the glass of frothy, faintly chocolate-colored liquid as though she weren't quite certain of her own words.

"I'll have one too," Falk told the soda fountain clerk. "And a ham sandwich. Want a sandwich?" he asked Teddi.

"No, thanks." Teddi bent her head to the straws and her heart began to hammer. She felt as gauche as a twelve-year-old, and couldn't think of a thing to say.

Mr. Falk drummed on the counter impatiently as he waited for the electric mixer to whip up his drink. Teddi noticed his fingers, as she always noticed everything about him. They were expressive, like his eyes.

"You're early today."

"I'm having exams," Teddi managed to reply.

"You're pretty keen on this dancing, aren't you?"

Teddi nodded, without being able to speak.

"Want to go on the stage?"

"I want to be a ballerina," Teddi said.

Falk seemed to be considering her. "You'd look well behind footlights," he murmured appraisingly as he started to sip his own drink. "A blonde can get that porcelain-angel look—" He bit into his ham sandwich and paused.

Teddi's heart did a flutter kick and turned over, but she didn't dare look up.

"More maturity, more training," Justin Falk sighed. "A few years in some ballet company. But it's a darned hard life."

Suddenly Teddi was afire. "I don't mind. I'll work!" she insisted. "Really I will."

The instructor seemed to be amused. "And then you'll fall in love with some nice young man from the suburbs and get married and have three children—" He shrugged. "And that will be that."

"I won't!" Teddi cried, incensed. Then she turned scarlet and her dark lashes dropped. "You're making fun of me."

"Believe me, I'm not!" Falk's voice rang with a sincerity equal to Teddi's, but there was an undercurrent of dismay that he had caused her embarrassment. "It's just that one gets so few dancers with appearance as well as talent. They're either stringy or fat or they have receding chins. Or," he added savagely, "they dance like cows."

Teddi knew that he was paying her a backhanded compliment, but she had become speechless again. Out of the corner of her eye she watched Falk finish his sandwich in moody silence. She couldn't ask the questions that raced in confusion through her head. Her heart had a captive-butterfly flutter that alarmed her and she felt as abject and devoted as either Sherry or Flip had ever looked.

Falk tossed some bills on the counter when he had finished eating and when Teddi took her wallet out of her coat pocket he waved it away. Grinning, he acknowledged her weak "Thank you," and said, "I'd buy a pretty girl a milk shake any day."

His voice was teasing, but Teddi kept repeating the words to herself. "Pretty girl," he'd said, not "pretty child." She didn't tell anyone, not even Cecile, about the encounter, but she remembered every detail with photographic clarity, and when she went into the small practice room to start work she was as self-conscious as Jane had been on the evening when she walked downstairs to greet Tommy.

As a consequence she danced badly. Her mind was divided, and she stumbled over combinations through which she had previously sailed. Justin Falk didn't spare her. He criticized her and scolded her as though he had never sat next to Teddi at the drugstore and indicated that he considered her a talented and attractive girl.

After class Cecile asked, "What was the matter with you today?" but Teddi just shrugged. Falk was always a demanding taskmaster and in the face of what had gone before, Teddi couldn't feel that his faultfinding had been more than superficial. She floated home on a private cloud and that evening she hunted through the drawers of her maple desk to find the old newspaper picture of Justin Falk in dancing costume and, with her bedroom door closed against Jane's sharp eyes, she stood looking at it for a long time.

Finally she got a pair of scissors and cut off the ragged edges carefully. Then she slipped it into her wallet behind her Athletic Association season ticket.

Midyear, for the next week, continued to drag along. There was a typical February cold snap, and the Spring Mill pond became coated with ice, so that most of the high school crowd spent every spare minute on skates.

Teddi, on the days when she didn't have dancing class, went along with the rest. She skated with the careless perfection of balance that indicated a trained dancer, and if she was feeling especially gay and frivolous, she would execute simple ballet steps on the tips of her skates.

Jane skated well too, having some of the same inherited sense of coordination. It was her favorite sport, and she cavorted around the ice like a frisky pup, her eyes sparkling and her cheeks wind-whipped to a cherry red.

"That kid sister of yours is getting awfully cute," Bill Bryant commented as he and Teddi stood for a moment watching the skaters on Thursday afternoon. "Better watch out, Teddi, she'll be stealing your men."

Teddi laughed, not in the least alarmed. She practically never had dates with anybody but Rod, and Rod had been faithful ever since the Harvest Hoedown, though now and then he would look at her with a peculiar expression and ask, "What are you dreaming about?"

Just then Jane skated by with Claire Woodward, who looked like a costume doll in her short skating skirt and head scarf.

"Hey, Teddi!" Jane called back over her shoulder. "Mother wants us to get home early. Remember?"

Teddi remembered. She looked at the new wristwatch which had been a Christmas present from Aunt Dora and called, "We'd better get going."

Jane was reluctant but agreeable. "I'll meet you by the bridge in five minutes," she called back.

While Teddi was sitting on a fallen log unlacing her shoe skates, Rod sauntered up. "Going home?" he asked.

To Teddi it seemed obvious. "But immediately!" she said.

Rod shifted feet. "Mind if I come along?"

"Of course not. I'm meeting Jane up by the bridge."

Rod looked a little chagrined, but not devastated. He slung Teddi's skates over his shoulder with his own, and scrambled beside her up the icy bank to the road.

Jane was leaning over the bridge, balancing herself on her stomach, and laughing down at some of the skaters below, but when she turned and saw that Rod was with Teddi, her expression suddenly changed.

"Hi," she said noncommittally, and marched along by Teddi's side in almost complete silence.

She scooted up the Baldwins' walk with a mumbled excuse, leaving Teddi to say a leisurely good-by to Rod and tell him yes, she'd be glad to go skating with him Saturday afternoon.

When Teddi came into the house, Jane was hanging her coat in the hall closet. "Why didn't you tell me Rod was bringing you home?" she whirled around to ask.

Teddi looked at her in astonishment. "But what difference did it make?"

Jane, however, flared right back. "D'you think I want to tag along feeling like a fifth wheel on a wagon?"

Teddi felt that she had every right to be annoyed. "Oh, Jane, act your age. Rod doesn't care if you're there or not. He just wanted to ask me to go skating Saturday afternoon."

But before Teddi had finished speaking, Jane was halfway upstairs. She ran into her room and banged the door.

Jane continued to be temperamental all through dinner. She kept her eyes moodily fixed on her plate and ate without apparent relish. She spoke when she was addressed or to say, "Please pass the biscuits," but she was barely polite.

Even when Mrs. Baldwin suggested that Saturday morning might be a good time to take the girls to Philadelphia on a long-promised shopping trip, she only grunted at the prospect.

Instead of dawdling, she raced through the dishes, then went into the living room and curled up in a chair with a library book while Teddi sat down at the desk and, after chewing her pencil for a while, wrote quickly:

Dear Pat,

You remember I told you about J. F.? (I don't want to write his name because he really is pretty famous and you never can tell who might know him.) Well, you know how he affects me—I mean, he really is the most super person I've ever known in my entire life.

Well, one day last week I was in the drugstore next to Valentin's having a milk shake and I looked up and there he was—on the stool right next to me!

Pat, I could have died. For a while I couldn't even think and then we began to have the most fascinating conversation. He thinks I have talent, Pat. He said so. And he said something else, too, sort of indirectly—

The telephone rang and Teddi looked up, but Jane unwound herself from the wing chair, picked up the receiver, and said, "Hello."

"Oh, hello, Claire." Her voice became a little brighter, then discouraged, as she said, "I'd love to, but I've lost my season ticket."

There was a comment from the other end of the wire, and Jane replied, "I don't know. Wait a minute." She covered the receiver with her hand and turned halfway around. "Teddi, you going to the basketball game tonight?"

"No, I'm not," Teddi murmured, forcing Jane to ask a second question.

"May I borrow your season ticket, then?"

"If you tie it around your neck with a string," Teddi retorted. "I don't want you to lose that too."

"O.K., I can go. I'll meet you in ten minutes."

Jane went upstairs to brush her hair and get her fur mittens, which she always reserved for special occasions. She came down again on the heels of her parents, who were dressed to go out, and called from the hall, "Where's that ticket, Teddi?"

Teddi had Flip on her lap. She was stroking her soft ears with one hand while the other was again flying across the paper. "In my wallet," she told Jane absently, "on the hall table." She went on writing, completely absorbed.

Suddenly there was a whoop from the hall, and Teddi looked up to see Jane just picking up a piece of paper that had fluttered from the wallet to the floor.

Teddi pushed back her chair and was across the floor in a flash, but she wasn't fast enough.

"Hey! Look at this!" Jane was saying boisterously. "Teddi's secret passion—some guy in tights!"

"Give it to me."

Teddi spoke between clenched teeth and snatched the newspaper picture out of Jane's fingers.

Jane, surprised by such unleashed fury, said, "Well, for Pete's sake—"

"Let me see, Teddi." Quietly, Mrs. Baldwin held out her hand. "Isn't this your dancing instructor?"

Teddi didn't meet her mother's eyes. "Yes."

Mrs. Baldwin handed Teddi the picture. "You can't blame Jane too much for misunderstanding—" she murmured with a smile that told Teddi she knew Jane had not misunderstood.

Chapter 17

On Saturday morning, at Wanamaker's, Mrs. Baldwin bought Teddi a gray wool jacket and skirt and Jane a sweater and some new shirts. In the flurry of shopping the girls forgot that they had been barely on speaking terms for the past two nights and a day. They were actually laughing together when they started up to the restaurant in the elevator. It was there that they met Mrs. Rutherford, who looked flushed and breathless and unusually upset.

"Agnes!" Mrs. Baldwin greeted her. "Come have lunch with us, can't you?"

"I'd love to, but I've got to meet John," she said, speaking of her husband, "in just half an hour. He has to go out to the Coast unexpectedly and he wants me to fly out with him."

"Wonderful! When?"

"This afternoon." Mrs. Rutherford's hands worked nervously on her handbag. "It's so unexpected. I've got matinee seats and everything--" She suddenly unsnapped the clasp of her purse and drew out a rectangular envelope. "Marthe, maybe you and one of the girls could use them. They're for that new musical at the Forrest. It would be a shame to let them go to waste."

A few minutes later the Baldwins were sitting at a table near the windows in the ninth-floor restaurant with two tickets before them, trying to decide what to do about the matinee and at the same time order lunch.

"You and Jane take them and go," Mrs. Baldwin suggested to Teddi. "I'm really rather tired."

But Jane shook her head. "I promised to meet Claire Woodward at the pond this afternoon. I borrowed fifty cents from her last night and I've got to pay her." She stopped, looked at Teddi, then said, "You can't go either. You made a date with Rod."

Teddi snapped her fingers. "Oh, bother!" Then she brightened. "You can tell him, Jane—or leave a note on the front door. He'll understand."

"Mother, can't I go with you? Rod won't mind. Really he won't!" Teddi appealed her case.

Mrs. Baldwin shrugged. "It's up to you, Teddi. I didn't make the date."

"Then I'm going. You let him know, Jane, like a lamb." She shook off a feeling of guilt and smiled at her younger sister. "I'll do something for you someday."

Jane's eyes darkened as they met Teddi's. "I'll tell him," she said, "but if you're sorry afterward, don't blame me."

Teddi laughed confidently. "I won't." She leaned back as the waitress placed her luncheon plate before her, then picked up her fork and began to attack her fruit salad happily.

"Just the other day Justin—I mean Mr. Falk—was talking about the ballet in this show. I think it's really *important* that I should see it. Besides, it'll be fun."

After lunch Mrs. Baldwin and Teddi wandered down Chestnut Street, window-shopping until matinee time. Teddi was in high spirits. She chattered brightly about plans for Madame Valentin's spring recital.

"It's going to be early this year, about the time of Pat's vacation, I think." Another thought occurred to her.

"Maybe she'll be able to come."

Teddi didn't know yet what she would be doing in the recital, but it was certain that pupils from Falk's classes would take leading parts.

"I hope he dances," Teddi told her mother. "He's marvelous—really he is! You just can't imagine until you've seen him."

"No," said her mother dryly, "I suppose I can't."

Joining the crowd about to enter the Forrest Theatre doors, Teddi stopped to look at the picture of the featured dancer on the billboards, tugging her mother's arm rapturously. "Isn't she beautiful?"

"Not beautiful, but very interesting," Mrs. Baldwin demurred. "She looks like a dancer."

"I know what you mean. So does Cecile." Teddi sighed. "I don't. I look too American, I guess." Her mind skipped ahead. "I ought to ask Cecile out to dinner, really I ought. When can I, Mother?"

Mrs. Baldwin was taking the tickets out of the printed envelope. "Why, any time. Maybe it would be fun to have a little supper party when Pat comes home. You could ask her then."

Teddi considered this as they entered the lobby, but she couldn't give it her full attention until she had wriggled out of her coat and was comfortably seated with a program in her hand.

"I don't know if Pat and Cecile would like each other, but it's an idea."

Mrs. Baldwin had timed their arrival well. They had barely five minutes to wait until the lights dimmed and the curtains parted on the opening chorus. From then on Teddi sat absorbed.

Hung on the thread of a trivial but brisk little story were songs and dance routines that were captivating and gay. Teddi followed every step of the chorus with fascination, because she knew enough to recognize their originality.

She thought the girls were sophisticated and beautiful, but the men seemed uninteresting and even looked a little jaded in their bright costumes. They could dance, though. She had to admit that.

The curtains closed for a second, and then parted to reveal the famous ballerina alone on the stage. There was something so dramatic, so exciting about the slender, poised figure, that Teddi's breath escaped in an audible sigh.

"Look! She's dancing in her bare feet," she whispered after a second. "Oh, I wish she had on toe shoes!"

"Maybe she'll dance again," Mrs. Baldwin whispered back. Then she too sat enthralled by the artistry of the dancer—by her grace, her nuances of interpretation, by the indefinable personality that made her great.

The patter song by the male lead which followed, and the chorus that closed the first act were lost on Teddi. She sat wrapped in dreams. To dance like that!

At intermission she would have sat on tranquilly, still dreaming, but her mother was restless, so Teddi followed her out to the lobby for a drink of water and a breath of fresh air.

There were a hundred people with the same idea, and the Baldwins soon found themselves caught in a crush.

"Goodness. Let's get out of this." Mrs. Baldwin started to work her way back through the crowd when a man's face, half turned toward her, gave her pause.

"Teddi," she asked in her ordinary, conversational tone of voice, "isn't that Mr. Falk?"

Justin Falk turned a split second after Teddi recognized him. He had heard his name spoken by the slender, rather striking woman in the beige suit. His eyes rested on her for a moment without recognition. Then he saw Teddi and he nodded and smiled.

Teddi was trapped. The mere presence of Justin Falk overwhelmed her and made the blood rush to her cheeks.

And seeing him in a strange environment was so totally unexpected that she had a mad desire to dodge out of sight.

"Mr. Falk, I'd like you to meet my mother," she nevertheless found herself saying feebly. "Mother—Mr. Falk."

Somehow, the dancing master didn't seem quite as presentable in his street clothes as he did in his easy, casual practice shirt and slacks. His suit needed pressing or he looked too slight or something. Teddi couldn't figure it out.

She didn't have long to try. Justin Falk was shaking her mother's hand, then turning to a woman who stood beside him, a brunet slightly taller than he. "Mrs. Baldwin, my wife."

Teddi couldn't believe her ears. She looked from Justin Falk to his companion, and the color drained from her face.

"And this is Theodora Baldwin—Teddi, we call her—one of my pupils."

Teddi mumbled the conventional "How do you do."

The second-act call bell buzzed, covering the weakness of her greeting, and Mrs. Falk had just time to say to Mrs. Baldwin, "Justin has told me about your daughter. He thinks she has real promise, and Justin seldom makes a mistake." Then they all turned and hurried back to their seats.

Teddi's knees would scarcely support her as she followed her mother down the aisle. She felt as though she were trying to walk through a nightmare. Her cheeks were burning and her heart was beating almost visibly.

"Interesting, isn't it, how small men so often marry women larger than themselves," Mrs. Baldwin was murmuring as she settled herself in her seat.

Teddi didn't reply.

"He seems very nice, though—Mr. Falk." Mrs. Baldwin glanced at her daughter shrewdly. "You didn't tell me he was married, or did you?"

"I guess I didn't." Teddi managed to reply as the curtain again went up.

Afterward, Teddi could recall nothing of the second act. She couldn't recall the songs that were sung, or remember the theme of the really exquisite ballet number which preceded the final curtain.

Shock was gradually replaced by mortification and an unwarranted sense of shame. Why, that woman was *old*. She was as old as Ginny Smith's sister; she was almost as old as Aunt Dora. It seemed incredible that such a person could be the wife of Justin Falk.

Her incomparable Justin! If she had been home, alone in the house, she could have lain on her bed and wept and beat the bedspread with her fists. But here no physical release was possible. Teddi was forced to sit and literally face the music of the comedy that tripped along so inconsequentially before her. Here she had to keep her chin up and her eyes dry. For she must never let her mother guess! She must never, never let anyone suspect for an instant that she could have been such a little idiot. Then, with a sick feeling in her stomach, she remembered that revealing letter to Pat!

I can fix that, she promised herself. I can act as though it were all just a big joke. But what if Pat should repeat the story? She could hear the gossip among the girls.

"—and you know that *awful* crush Teddi Baldwin had on her dancing master—before she found he was married—oh, haven't you *heard?*"

Teddi sat with her hands clenched in her lap, feeling sick at her stomach. Somehow, she would have to keep Pat from telling. Somehow—

She wished she had never come. She wished she had gone on home and kept her date with Rod. The thought of Rod made her feel even more wretched.

Mrs. Baldwin was applauding and the curtain was closing, then opening again for the leads to take their calls. Teddi clapped automatically, but the exercise didn't warm her hands.

"Well, that was entertaining," her mother was saying as

she shrugged into her coat. "And the music was really delightful. I'll have to do something nice for Agnes Rutherford. It was a very pleasant afternoon."

"Yes, it was," Teddi managed, with a thin smile. She wanted to push past all the people who were clogging the aisle and get out of the theater and out of Philadelphia and home, but she was forced to walk sedately behind her mother, taking one careful step at a time.

On the street it was better. The late afternoon air was cold and damp and the walk to the station was refreshing. Teddi and Mrs. Baldwin bent their heads against the wind and talked little, and by the time they were on the train Teddi had recovered her equilibrium sufficiently to conduct a conversation in a voice that wouldn't betray her inward agitation. At least that is what she thought.

Mrs. Baldwin made it easy for her. She bought an evening paper and gave the back section to Teddi, whose eyes roved blindly over the comics.

"I think I'll call up Rod and apologize," she told her mother after a while. "I suppose it was kind of mean to run out on him. Do you think he'll be mad?"

"I don't know. Rod seems like a pretty amenable boy—up to a point. I guess it's up to you to find out when that point will be reached."

Teddi didn't answer. She sat with the newspaper in front of her wishing that the sinking sensation would go away. She had never felt more forlorn.

Through her flashed a desire to unburden all her woes to her mother, to make a clean breast of everything as she had when she was a child. But she wasn't a child now, any more than she was a woman. Now she was possessed of a pride that kept her silent.

The walk home through the February dusk was short. The house was ablaze with lights and George Baldwin was wandering about aimlessly.

"Marthe!" he called the minute the front door opened,

and came to help her off with her coat and follow her out to the kitchen while she put some potatoes in the oven to bake.

Teddi went upstairs, washed her hands and brushed her hair, and came down again to call Rod.

"He isn't home, Teddi," Mrs. Shaw said when she answered the phone. "I think I remember his saying he was going skating with you."

Teddi put down the receiver and went upstairs again, into her dark bedroom and across to the window that looked down on the front walk. It seemed stuffy in the house, and her cheeks still felt hot. She raised the window a few inches and dropped to her knees to lean against the sill.

From somewhere up the street came the sound of voices, then a trill of laughter that was unmistakably Jane's. Teddi couldn't see her sister, but she could hear her feet, running toward the house, and the jingle of her skates slapping together on her back.

Someone was with her—a boy—and the two of them were playing "last tag," racing back and forth from the walk to the drive next door in absorbed glee. Suddenly Teddi leaned forward in the darkness. That chuckle sounded like Rod! A car's headlights picked out a figure. It was Rod!

Teddi scrambled to her feet, ready to raise the window and call out, just as Rod tagged Jane again. This time he caught and held her arm. "I've got to go now, but what about skating tomorrow?"

Teddi could almost hear Jane's laughter die. "You mean —along with Teddi?"

"The heck with Teddi," Rod said roughly. "I ought to've seen, long before this, that she has other fish to fry."

"I don't know—I'm not sure—" Jane's voice was troubled as she backed toward the gate.

"Will you call me?" Rod persisted.

"Yes, I'll call you." A moment later the front door

banged, Jane's skates were dropped on the hall floor, and Jane herself came slowly up the stairs.

Teddi had turned on the light and closed the window by the time her sister entered her room. She stood in front of the mirror humming a snatch of tune and running the brush in long sweeps through her hair.

Reflected in the glass, Jane's face had never before seemed so alive and glowing. Her lips were parted and her cheeks and the tip of her nose were apple-red.

"Teddi," she said at once, "when Rod found you weren't here he asked me to go along instead, and I went. Was that all right?"

"But of course!" Teddi laughed and turned around, compelling her eyes to sparkle, her voice to sound approving. "Maybe you can take Rod off my hands."

"He wants us to go skating tomorrow," Jane said.

Teddi yawned, covering her mouth with the back of her hand. "You go," she said, though it cost her a tremendous effort. "I've got a bad blister from my toe shoes and I just can't bear the thought of putting on my skates."

"You don't really mind if I go with Rod?"

"Mind?" Teddi's voice rose perilously but she brought it under control and laughed again. "Of course I don't mind. Rod's a nice boy and I think we should sort of keep him in the family, but that's the only feeling I have."

Chapter 18

On the evening of the Valentin School recital Teddi Baldwin stood waiting in the wings.

"Nervous, Teddi?" Justin Falk asked as he passed her on feet as light and quiet as a cat's, bent on collecting and calming the scattered corps de ballet.

"A little," Teddi admitted, with an eerie feeling that she had stood in this spot and that she had been asked this question before. Then she remembered. It had been on the evening of the hospital benefit when she had danced with the children of the Heritage School. "Nervous?" Miss Heritage had asked, and Teddi had made the same reply.

Yet aside from this haunting repetition of circumstance, the other evening seemed long, long ago. Teddi could look back on the garden party and smile when she thought of how flattered she had been by Jill Martin's rapturous admiration. Why, she had been a mere child herself!

"The audience is really *big*."

Cecile, in the costume of the Snow Queen from *The Nutcracker* came back from the stage, where she had been peering through a peephole in the curtain. Her eyes were rounder than usual and she kept wetting her dry lips.

'Good," Teddi said, unsurprised. It was a beautiful night, more like May than the end of March, and Madame

Valentin had advertised her recital well. Besides the usual quota of ballet mammas there would be uncles and aunts and cousins and friends who might not have been lured out on a rainy evening. There might also, because Valentin's was a professional school, be some talent scouts. It was an exciting possibility to consider. It even made a little shiver chase up Teddi's spine.

"I saw Mother and Father," Cecile said.

"Did you? Where are they?"

Teddi moved across the stage to take her turn at the peephole, behind which there were now other dancers in line.

"On the right, about six rows back," Cecile told her, but when Teddi put her eye to the opening it was her own mother she saw first. She and her father were just sitting down, and Jane was coming down the aisle, looking quite self-possessed in spite of the fact that she was responsible for two escorts, Rod Shaw and Bill Bryant. Bill, Teddi noticed, looked uncommonly attractive in a sports coat and brown slacks. She was glad he was here, though she'd been surprised, Saturday night, when he had asked if she would mind if he bought a ticket and came along with Jane and Rod.

"Of course not. I'd be pleased!" Teddi had laughed. "But don't be too sure Rod's coming. He had an overdose of ballet last fall and he may be off it for life."

Bill shook his head. "He wants to see you dance. He told me. He still thinks you're the McCoy, you know."

"Only he's more *comfortable* with Jane. I know." Teddi had smiled without malice, surprised to find that she was even rather glad that Rod was dating Jane. It had given Jane a new self-confidence of which Teddi approved.

"Hey! It's my turn now!" a voice at Teddi's ear complained. She stepped quickly back from the curtain, remembering too late that she had not yet discovered Mr. and Mrs. Perrine in the audience.

"Sorry," she apologized, then went back to explain to Cecile.

But in the usual preperformance confusion Cecile had disappeared. Teddi finally found her in the dressing room where Mrs. Falk was putting finishing touches on the makeup of a little girl of eleven.

"I smeared my left eyebrow," Cecile explained, "and I came to get it fixed."

Teddi waited while Victoria Falk redrew Cecile's brow. "Now keep your hands away from your face," the wife of the dancing master cautioned, "or you'll disgrace me. To say nothing of the Valentin School. We can't have the Snow Queen look as if she's fallen in the coal bin, can we, Teddi?"

Teddi grinned. Cecile looked so chaste, with her hair like dark wings against the white of her headdress and her costume, that the suggestion was as absurd as Mrs. Falk knew it to be.

"Cecile always pulls at her eyebrows when she's upset," she replied. "You'd better check up on her the last minute before she's to go on."

Madame stuck her head in the door. "All set, Vicky?"

"All set. Do they look all right?"

"Fine. Fine." Madame, hearing the first strains of the lilting music being played by the three-piece orchestra, hurried to a wing, and the children who were dressed as guests for the Christmas party crowded before her. Three minutes later the curtains parted and *The Nutcracker* began.

Justin Falk himself, in harlequin costume and a square, high headdress, danced the Nutcracker doll come to life. Teddi watched from the wing and thought, as she had thought during every rehearsal, that she had never seen anything so pointed and clear as his pantomime. When he led the child, in a dream, to the land of the Snow Queen, he carried the audience with him, and made every scene more vital for his presence, even made imperfections in the ensemble less obvious, because he was there.

Cecile, as the Snow Queen, was dainty and precise. Her eyebrows remained unsmudged, and she danced with what Teddi considered great elegance. The applause after her exit expressed the pleasure of the house. The onlookers could instinctively recognize a budding ballerina when they saw one, and they saw one in Cecile.

While the snow set was being changed and the fat red and white striped pillars that represented candy canes were being rolled into place for the next scene, Teddi congratulated her friend.

"Someday you'll have your name in lights," she told her.

Cecile was flattered, but she shook her head. "It is best not to look ahead, but to continue to work very hard."

It was Teddi's turn to shake her head. "You're incorrigible," she said, but even though she teased her, she understood Cecile because they felt much the same about their dancing. In ballet they knew there was no shortcut to fame.

"Teddi! Oh, there you are!"

Teddi walked away from Cecile to stand beside Justin Falk for the few seconds before the curtains parted again on the Kingdom of Sweets.

"You all right?"

"Sure."

"Remember, if you get dizzy on those final turns, just pull in and stop. The pianist will take your cue."

"I think I can manage." Teddi had begged to be allowed to dance the professional routine for the Sugarplum Fairy number, instead of using the simplified score Mr. Falk had prepared for the recital as a whole. She smiled up at the dancing instructor with all the confidence she could muster, and he nodded and grinned back, then adjusted his headdress and prepared to go on.

It seemed incredible to Teddi that the admiration she now felt for Justin Falk could have taken the turn it had in those weeks before that day at the theater. She could not imagine why his mere presence could ever have made her heart leap and pound, the color flood to her cheeks.

She was glad, in a way, that Pat's spring vacation had not coincided with the time of the recital after all, and that she couldn't be here. Because for all Falk's vibrant stage personality, for all his exquisite dancing and miming, Pat never, never would have understood. It was better that the dancing master should remain only a mirage in Pat's mind. Then she would never have the chance to say, "But, Teddi! How could you have been such a silly? Why, he's old!"

Teddi dipped the tips of her toe shoes into rosin, then made way for the girl who was to dance the Arabian. She adjusted the crown of the Sugarplum Fairy on her shining hair, smoothed the basque of her silver-spangled pink tutu, and fluffed out the tulle ruffles that were attached to the back of her shoulder straps like little wings.

"Ready, Teddi?" she heard Madame hiss.

With the opening note of the Dance of the Sugarplum Fairy, Teddi left the wing.

The moment she was on the stage and dancing she was conscious of the quick response and warmth of the audience. On the night of the hospital benefit Teddi had danced for herself alone, intoxicated by a newfound sense of freedom, scarcely conscious of the reaction of the guests seated on folding chairs beyond the footlights.

But tonight the enthusiasm of the audience filled Teddi with a responsive glow. It made her want to give these gracious people the very best of which she was capable. It made her want to be worthy, as she wanted to be worthy of her family.

As she executed the pas de bourré, the developpés, and posés of the swift, gay little dance, she felt that she was drawing strength and sureness from those who watched her —from her mother and father, from Jane, from Rod and Bill, from Justin Falk on the stage beside her, from Cecile and Madame in the wings, and from the dim, unknown faces upturned appreciatively. She was no longer dancing alone.

And then she was swept by a certainty more deep and definite than ever before, a rooted knowledge that asked no questions. This was the life for her.

Madame said a ballerina needed an indefinable something called personality. Very well. It would come. It was already coming, through the very process of living. Justin Falk was giving it to her, and Jane, and Rod and her mother. Heartache and achievement and the slow process of growing up were all contributing. When the time arrived, it would be there.

The tempo of the music quickened, and Teddi began the final pas de chat, pas de bourrée turns.

She was breathing hard now, concentrating only on spotting.

One—two—three.

She did two quick piqués arabesques and a finish. Then applause was sweeping through the house and she was bowing and smiling and running off the stage to make way for the intermediate class pupils who were to dance the Waltz of the Flowers.

Beyond, the applause continued, and Madame hugged Teddi with Latin exuberance and turned her around.

"Better take a curtain call, Teddi," she said.

About the Author

BETTY CAVANNA, author of more than seventy books for young people, grew up in Haddonfield, New Jersey, and majored in journalism at Douglass College. She holds an honorary membership in Phi Beta Kappa from the Rutgers University Chapter for her outstanding contribution to the field of juvenile literature.

Miss Cavanna worked on newspapers and in advertising, before devoting her talents to writing about young people. Among her books is the all-time best seller, *Going on Sixteen,* which has sold more than a million copies and which has been translated into several languages. The author resides in Concord, Massachusetts.

Cavanna, Betty 6024
Cav
Ballet fever

MEISTER ELEMENTARY LIBRARY